Thank you so much ♥
Michele
J.M.M. Adams

SOPHIA and the DRAGON

A Sophia and Kanani Mystery

By J.M.M. ADAMS

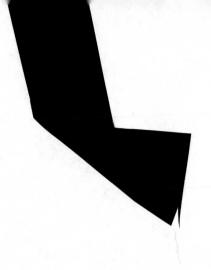

ACKNOWLEDGEMENTS

Dragon Artist: Steven J. Catizone

Editor: Richard Perfrement

Titles by J.M.M. ADAMS

Kanani's Golden Caves

Sophia and the Stradivarius

(Appearing in *First String* this year at the Indie Film Festivals

in Asia, Europe, World Wide.)

Sophia and the Dragon

The Russian Spy

The Mystery of Sandy Island

The Mystery of St. Moritz

Be sure to check out Michele's other books at

   www.jmmadams.com

   http://amzn.to/2bhoEcZ

This book is Dedicated to all
Canines in the military, police dept.,
and other departments; keeping us
safe from evil.
May God always look over
them with protection
and love.

CONTENTS

SOPHIA AND THE DRAGON

Sophia Anderson (From Hawaii, Port Townsend, WA and Luxembourg 2013) Nickname is Sophie.

Kanani (Sophia's long haired German Shepherd)

John Barnes (Sophia's deceased husband)

Susan and Kimo (Good Friends)

Leila (Sophia's niece)

Jennie (Sophia's sister that disappeared in Egypt through time travel, Leila's mother)

Richard (Jennie's husband that disappeared with her)

Yglais (Mother of Lamorak and Perceval)

Lamorak (Knight of the Round Table, Knight that found Sophia, he was more famous than Gawain.

Perceval (Knight of the Round Table and brother of Lamorak)

Cundrie (Witch, Accolon's wife, cousin to Lamorak and Perceval)

Accalon (Knight of the Round Table and husband to Cundrie)

Bryn (Maid to Sophia in 1180 AD)

Afawen (Maid to Sophia in 1180 AD)

Iago (Page in 1180 AD)

Ivis (The Head Cook at Lamorak's Castle 1180)

Gunther (White Dragon)

Drake (White Dragon)

JMM ADAMS

1

"SOPHIE!" Susan screams as Sophia disappears into the opening of the cave.

"Kanani no! Come back!" Leila called too late. Susan and Leila watch Kanani vanish through the portal.

Sophia tumbled through darkness for a long moment, then landed awkwardly and tumbled to the ground. She didn't know what had happened to her, so she looked around. She was on the ground beside a dirt road; across the road to her right was what looked like an English Pub. There was a bit of haze with the sun shining through and the air was humid, she could feel her hair starting to frizz around her face.

She thought to herself; *did I just go through time? This is unbelievable. I thought I could do that in Egypt?*

She struggled to her feet only to be knocked down again when Kanani tumbled from the portal, crashing into the back of her knees.

"Kanani, I'm glad to see you too and that you love me so much. I love you even more! Now can you please stop jumping back and forth over me?" She begged her German Shepherd as she struggled to stand back up.

I love you too Sophie, I'm just so happy to see you. Thought Kanani, as she licked Sophie's face.

Sophia stood up and straightened out her jean skirt, dusting off her black t-shirt.

Look out Sophie! There's a strange person approaching us. Kanani was barking warning Sophia.

Sophia heard a horse and looked up. Someone tall rode a big, black stallion towards them. As the rider drew near, Sophia caught the pale glint of sunlight off chain armor. He stopped in front of them and dismounted. He looked in his late twenties, about Sophia's age. He took his helmet off and tucked it under his arm. His long sandy blond hair fell out from under it. He was about six feet tall with a muscular build and the most beautiful blue eyes She had ever seen.

"Stop barking Kanani," Sophia scolded her German Shepherd.

Kanani stopped barking, *Ok, Sophie, but he better not hurt us.*

"Good day Madam, are you alright?"

"Yes, yes, I think so, thank you for stopping to ask." Sophia stuttered as she continued looking around, still wondering where they were. It looked a lot like Cornwall, but not the Cornwall she was familiar with.

"Who are you?"

"I'm Sophia and this is Kanani, we were exploring caves with my friends and ended up here. May I ask who you are and where I am?"

"Yes, my Lady it is the year of our Lord, 1180, you are in the County of Devon and I am Sir Lamorak de Gales. I am a Knight of the Round Table in King Arthur's court.

"May I pet your animal, Lady?" he asked without waiting for Sophia to answer him. He bent over to pet Kanani. Sophia was so glad Kanani didn't bite him.

"If she lets you pet her it's ok with me," Sophia managed to say.

I guess if he pets me he's ok Sophie. Kanani wagged her tail.

"I've never seen a dog like this and I have never seen anyone dressed like you." Said sir Lamorak.

Yeah, we've never seen anyone dressed like you either buddy, Kanani was saying with her tongue hanging out of her mouth.

Sophia's heart was beating so fast she was sure he could hear it.

Here I was dressed like a person from my time, at least I had leggings under my shirt. My hair probably didn't look bad, it was long, dark blonde and braided. Was I really standing here talking to a handsome knight? Sophia thought to herself.

"My dog is an Alsatian," Sophia hoped that would be less confusing than German Shepherd.

"Where are you from?" He asked studying her more closely.

"I'm from Luxembourg. But I'm from the year of our Lord 2013," She whispered.

"Did you say 2013? Did you come here on purpose? I don't understand how that happened." He looked amazed.

"No, it was an accident. I'm lost and really want to go back now!" She was unsure of herself and looked back at the rock she and Kanani apparently came through. The portal was not visible to her now though.

He followed her gaze and apparently saw nothing but a rock either.

Kanani looked too and walked over to the rock sniffing. Yeah, I can't believe we came through that either. Sophie sure does some fun things.

"I do not know how to get you back." He took note of dusk starting to fall. You must come to my Castle, I am not going to let a beautiful young lady and dog stand here all night for thieves to rob and kill."

"Your Castle? I don't have anything proper to put on for a castle visit," She looked down her skirt again, at least she wasn't in shorts!

"I'm sure my mother can find something for you to wear." He said then bent over and gently took her hand, giving it a kiss. Wow, I'll follow you anywhere. Sophia was thinking with a lump in her throat. She was still wondering how she would get back home. She felt a bit of dread in the pit of her stomach as he led her towards his castle.

"Will you remember where you found us?" She asked a bit pleadingly.

"Yes, I will." He turned to look at Sophia, "It's almost dark, and we must hurry."

Sophia grabbed her pack and took Kanani's leash out snapping it on her collar. He walked leading his horse behind them.

Would Susan and Leila get Kimo and come find us? Oh, I shouldn't have listened to Leila and I should have stayed home working on Grandpa's notes in my library in Luxembourg.

Sophia was choking back tears. She was having a hard time letting go since John, her husband, had been killed almost a year ago.

"What is that you have on your dog?" He interrupted Sophia's self-pity.

"It's called a leash; I don't think it's invented yet."

"No, it isn't, I have a lot of questions for you. Don't worry. You will be safe in my care, my Lady."

"I hope so," Sophia answered down cast.

We'll be ok Sophie, he's ok and I'm here with you. Kanani was walking close to Sophie and looking up at her.

As they advanced down the road Sophia looked around, the countryside was green with rolling hills. She decided to try and enjoy her predicament, since she was on this adventure whether She wanted to be or not.

I don't have anything to worry about. Susan and Kimo will take care of Leila and the house in Luxembourg. It is so beautiful here and looks very different from how I remembered it when Jennie and I came here on summer vacations with our Grandma and Grandpa. The farms and roads weren't here now, it was untouched. Being summer, the weather was nice and Kanani didn't seem upset by our recent experience. So, I might as well enjoy my adventure. It would be something else to write about when I got home. Sophia was telling herself.

After walking for about an hour Lamorak pointed at a castle and said with pride in his voice. "There's my castle."

"Wow, it's gorgeous!" Sophia was getting excited forgetting her predicament. She was a bit anxious to meet his family though.

"She has been in my family many years. When my father was slain in battle it became mine, which was five years ago. I now take care of my mother, Lady Yglais." He looked thoughtful.

"I don't think it's a good idea for anyone to know where you have come from, at least not today. My mother will wonder if she sees the way you are dressed. I will put you into a spare bedchamber right away, and then go find her. I will mention I met you, but not tell Her where you came from."

He was still talking, but he lost Sophia's attention, because they had just entered the most magnificent castle she had ever seen! They were walking through the courtyard no one was about.

She followed him into the stables. He handed his horse over to a page. The page looked at Sophia with suspicion but didn't say anything.

"Oh, he gives me the chills, he is staring at me Sir Lamorak."

"Never mind him. Come let's get you and your dog into the castle."

He pushed her gently in front of him to leave the stable. Then Kanani and Sophia followed Lamorak into the main hall of the castle. She tried looking around at everything without tripping, but had a hard time, because He was moving her rapidly to their room. They got there and He opened up the doors.

"This will be your chamber, please go in quickly." Lamorak told her.

She looked around at the beautiful room; there was a bed, washstand and a window looking out over the moors.

Yahoo, this is a neat pad Sophie. Check out that bed! Kanani bounded into to the room jumping on the bed, and then jumped off.

"Well your dog likes the room," laughed Lamorak.

"Make yourself comfortable and I will have some dresses and clothing brought in for you, my Lady. Don't be frightened, are you?"

"Not so much frightened, as concerned if I will be accepted. Then there's that little thing about how long I'll be here." She pinched herself, *yep, she was awake, and this was not a dream.* He saw her pinching herself.

"I don't understand how you got here, but everything will work out. I am pleased that I was the one that found you. This will put some excitement into our lives," he said with a bid of glee in his voice, and then he grinned turning around to walk out the door. He stopped remembering something, turned back to her around said; "I will escort you to dinner in two hours."

"Great, thank you."

Then he closed the door and disappeared.

"Doesn't he suspect I were going to try and get back home?" She said to Kanani as she took off her backpack and looked inside to see what Susan had loaded into it that morning.

No, I don't think so Sophie, but don't worry this is fun. Kanani looked in the bag with Sophia. She found the phone Grandpa had given her for the planned time travel in Egypt.

She had planned on going back in time to try to find her sister and brother -in -law. Jennie had disappeared over a year ago while on an excavation trip with her husband and Leila. Leila had stayed behind in the camp that morning. They never returned to her. That's how Leila had come to live in Luxembourg under Sophia's care. Grandpa had told her this phone worked for time travel; well she was going to give it a test after getting cleaned up. She felt and looked grubby and dirty. She walked over to the basin of water and washed her face, then looked into the mirror sighing. Of course, she had no makeup in her pack. She was going to miss a lot of things. A knock at the door startled her.

"Come in."

The door opened, and a young maid walked in carrying ten gowns, then another one followed her carrying more clothes. They were gorgeous gowns; Sophia couldn't believe it!

"Look at those dresses! I am so thankful; I don't know what to say except thank you."

"You're very welcome Lady," said the first maid. "I will hang them up in the closet; do you need anything else or help with anything my Lady?"

"Yes, I need to know what to wear to dinner tonight, and I need some face stuff to make me pretty."

"Afawen," she pointed to the other girl, "put some makeup over there for you by the basin, if you need other colors let me know. There is also some lotion with it, would you like some hot water to be brought in for a bath?"

"I would love that so much!" Exclaimed Sophia.

"Ok, my name is Bryn and we will be back soon," but instead of leaving she walked over to the hanging gowns and pulled one out. "This blue one would look very nice on you tonight." She said holding it up for inspection.

It was the most gorgeous blue gown Sophia had ever seen. "Thank you. That one will do fine. It's nice to meet you Bryn. My name is Sophia; my friends call me Sophie."

"Your welcome, I will be here to assist you for your stay. Then she giggled, looking down at Kanani. May I pet her? She's so pretty."

"Yes, let me introduce you to Kanani." Sophia walked over and knelt by her dog, then invited Bryn to come over and pet her.

"Thank you, my Lady," then she stood up. "I'll be back with your hot water very soon." She turned and walked out of the room.

"What an endearing young lady." Sophia said to Kanani and then sighed, "This might be fun, I'm going to try and call Grandpa."

Kanani was looking around the room and thinking, *Not bad for a place to stay. I wonder where we are? Yes, Sophie, this will be fun, Woof woof!*

Sophia knew that Susan and Leila were probably frantic that she and Kanani had disappeared.

Picking up the phone She dialed the number Grandpa had given her. It rang only once to her great relief. She heard his voice on the other end of it.

"Hello. Sophie is this you my dear?"

"Hi Grandpa. Yes, it's me and I want you to know that I am ok and it's so nice to hear your voice!"

"It's nice to hear your voice too, my dear. Susan and Kimo called telling me about your disappearance right after it happened. They were very upset, but I calmed them down. We'll figure out how to get you home. What year did you land in sweetheart?"

"I landed in 1180 and I'm staying at Sir Lamorak de Gales castle in Devon, England. He is a knight in King Arthur's court, can you Google him Grandpa, and let me know whatever you can find out about him?" She pleaded.

"Yes, dear I can do that for you. Are they treating you like the princess you are to me?" The warmth in his voice quieted her.

"Yes, Grandpa they are; I have ten beautiful gowns hanging in my wardrobe! Lamorak acts like I'm here to stay forever!"

"Well, sweetheart this is good for you to have a little adventure. I want you to start living again after your heartache of losing John," he told her endearingly.

"I know Grandpa, but this is strange, oh, someone is knocking on my door; I'll call you back tomorrow. Please let everyone know I'm ok. I love you Grandpa."

"Ok, sweetheart I will, and I love you too," then he hung up.

Sophia tossed the phone in her pack and hurried over to open the door. The castle attendants were carrying her bath water, soap and anything else she needed. They filled the tub and as they were leaving Bryn walked in.

"Well it looks in place, my Lady. Can I be of help with your bath or help you dress?"

"Yes, could you come back in thirty minutes and help me with the dress? I would be grateful."

"Yes, I can, now enjoy your hot bath my Lady and I will be back soon." Bryn left closing the door behind her.

"I will," shouted Sophia after her.

It looked like a lovely bath, Sophia peeled off her dirty clothes, folding them and placing them in her pack. Then she stepped into the hot inviting bath. It felt good on her aching muscles and she relaxed. Not having much time, because Bryn would be back soon, she got out and dried off. She was just slipping the dress on when there was a knock on the door.

"Bryn, is that you?"

"Yes, my lady. May I come in now?" She asked.

"Yes, I'm ready for you."

She entered and asked, "How was your bath?"

"Fantastic! It picked up my spirit and I needed that."

"Good," she helped button up the dress and apply face color. When they were all done Bryn looked at her.

"You look lovely, my Lady. Yes, you will do."

"Really? Thank you so much!" Sophia gave Bryn a hug, which made her blush.

"I will make sure Kanani is fed, what does she eat?" Bryn asked.

Well, as long as she feeds me what I like, come on Sophie, tell her what I like to eat. Kanani was thumping her tail at Bryn.

"She can eat meat and needs drinking water. I would really appreciate that, thank you." Sophia said.

"Your welcome, I'll be back after you go to dinner and take care of her."

"Thank you again Bryn," then she left. Sophia hugged Kanani; she just cocked her and gave Sophia a look.

"We're going to be ok, sweetie. Bryn will come back with your food and take you out for potty. I love you Nani!" Sophia buried her face into Kanani's neck.

I love you too, don't be gone too long. Kanani didn't want her to leave at all.

Then there was a knock on the door, letting go of Kanani Sophia walked over and opened it up. Handsome Sir Lamorak was standing there!

"Good evening," Sophia said, "do you like how I look now?" She asked him to twirl around.

Then she really looked at him, he was so handsome in his blue linen shirt and black pants. The blue shirt brought out the blue of his eyes. Oh, she could fall for him.

"You are very beautiful my Lady," he replied, "I am honored to escort you to dinner." Then he stuck out his arm for Sophia to take hold of. She looked back at Kanani and told her to be a good girl. That she would be back soon. Sophia was really nervous.

They walked into the dining room. Everyone was already seated.

"Mother, I would like to introduce you to Lady Sophia of Luxembourg," Lamorak stepped back to show off Sophia and introduce her to his mother. She was shocked he called her that, how was she going to pull this one off?

"Very nice to meet you Lady Yglais," she said with a curtsy.

"It's very nice to meet you as well, let me introduce you to everyone, my dear." Lady Yglais continued. She pointed as she spoke, "The man to my left is my other son, Perceval; next to him is Accalon and then his wife Cundrie. Accalon is my nephew and both he and his wife are staying here with us for the time being. Why don't you sit here next to me on my right, dear?" She patted the seat next to her.

"Hello, it's nice to meet all of you," Sophia said, then turned to Yglais, Lamorak's mother, "I am honored to sit next to you my Lady, thank you."

Lamorak pulled out the chair and she sat down. Sophia made it through dinner without any mishaps. Stories were told about the quests the knights had been on. Then she heard about how King Arthur had called everyone into his Kingdom for a festival starting tomorrow. Cundrie talked about what clothes to pack, Lady Yglais said that everyone should get up early, because the wagons needed to be packed up. Lady Yglais told Sophia that she was invited to go with them. Then the conversation changed and she asked Sophia if she loved children. Sophia told her yes, that she wanted to open a school someday. Lady Yglais thought that was a great idea. Sophia didn't mean for her to think she was opening one here! They talked about that for a while. After dinner was over the Page, Iago came in and gestured for Cundrie to leave and talk to him. Sophia wondered what that was about. No one else seemed to bother about it, so Sophia let it go.

Lamorak and his mother walked Sophia back to her room talking about what she needed to take for the trip to Camelot.

Sophia was a bit anxious how Kanani had done without her. She opened the door to her room, turned to say goodnight and thanked both of them for the lovely evening.

"I'll see you early in the morning, goodnight kind sir."

"Good night Lady Yglais, thank you for your hospitality."

"Good night my Lady," Lamorak and his mother both said, then they turned to walk away.

Sophia closed the door and screamed!!!!

2

THEY HEARD HER and Lamorak and ran back to Sophia's room. He thrust the door open and grabbed ahold of Sophia. Looking around he saw what she was so upset about.

"Who did this?" Sophia cried, running over to her backpack. She started throwing everything out; *my phone is missing!!!! All of my lovely dresses have been slashed, but that was nothing compared to losing my phone."* Sophia was devastated.

"I have a pretty good idea," said Lamorak angrily.

Bryn walked in with Kanani. Kanani ran over and jumped up on Sophia crying.

It's ok; really don't' cry. I'm here for you. Kanani started kissing Sophia.

"Thank you Kanani." Sophie sniffled.

"What happened? We were just here half an hour ago! This is horrible! Let me go get some help and we will get this cleaned up for you, my Lady." Then Bryn ran out of the room.

"Thank you," Sophia called after her as she sat down on her bed, she was upset.

"How can we ever get in touch with Grandpa again Kanani?" Sophia talked to her dog.

You have me; we have each other. Kanani kissed her again.

After everything was cleaned up, Lamorak insisted on sleeping outside the door of her chambers that evening to make her feel safe.

"Remember, Sophia, we go to Camelot tomorrow and you have traveled along way today. You need to feel safe tonight. Try and sleep." Then he closed the door and sat down on his cot to get comfortable for the night. *If I could just survive until that time, I would be happy.*

Sophia slept fitfully, tossing and turning. she couldn't believe this was happening to her. Maybe when she woke up, she'd be back home in her own bed. Perhaps this was a bad dream. At least Kanani was here snuggling up to her.

3

THE NEXT MORNING Lamorak was up before Sophia and had taken Kanani out for a walk.

Thank goodness Lamorak heard me whining at the door to go out. Then he took me into the big kitchen and the ladies fed me. Thought Kanani.

Sophia was up and dressed in the only dress not shredded when he came back.

"Good Morning Sophia, how are you this morning?"

"I'm fine and ready to go to Camelot, how are you?" Sophia asked going over and hugging Kanani.

"Me too, my mother found some more dresses for you, so we are all packed. Here is something for you to eat," he said.

Bryn walked in and placed a tray of cheese and crackers on Sophia's small round oak table placed under the window.

"Kanani and I already ate. You don't have much in here to take, but let Bryn help you after you eat."

"Thank you," she said to Bryn and Lamorak both, sitting down and taking a bite. She tossed Kanani a cracker.

That's nice! How about a second one?

"Kanani, stop begging young lady!" Lamorak said sternly.

Darn, he won't be easy to fool.

When she was full they helped her pack, they left the room and Lamorak loaded her things into the carriage.

"You are riding with my Mother and Cundrie, then Bryn and Afawen will be in the carriage behind you. Don't give Cundrie any information. She is a witch or thinks she is; I think she had something to do with ransacking your room last night. She is on to you somehow and it enrages her not knowing how you got here." Lamorak warned Sophia.

"Kanani and I will be our best behavior," she told him with a grin, then mounted the steps to the carriage with Kanani on her heels.

No way is Sophie going without me. Kanani was not letting Sophie out of her site!

Lamorak just cracked a smile and shook his head. He had never met a woman like this before; it was a challenge for him.

Sophia thought it was exciting looking out the window watching the horses ahead of them, then looking back seeing Lamorak, Perceval and Accalon in full armor riding their horses dressed in Camelot colors.

Yglais was knitting and Cundrie was staring out the window not paying any attention to either of them. Sophia hoped it stayed like that. Kanani was on the floor by Sophia's feet. The ladies only made a small fuss about having a dog in the carriage, actually Yglais was fine with it, Cundrie was the one that voiced her opinion. Finally, Yglais started talking to Sophia not looking up from her project.

"Lady Sophia, we can talk about the school now that we have some time. There are many children of different ages around us with no one to give them proper instruction. What will you need to get started?" Yglais asked her. The night before they had discussed opening a school.

"Well I need something to write on to teach them the alphabet so they will be able to read. For the younger children I have a more hands on way of teaching." Sophia answered her.

"Cundrie you can get something for Sophia to start teaching, I want you to be VERY helpful to her and not give her any grief." Stated Yglais sternly looking up in Cundrie's direction.

"Hmm," said Cundrie looking up at her. I apologize I was daydreaming and didn't hear what you two were talking about. Would you mind repeating the conversation?"

Boy Sophie don't trust that person. I'm going to have to watch Cundrie. Kanani stared at Cundrie.

Yglais shook her head in disgust and repeated what they had just discussed.

"I'm sure I can find all of the supplies you need. I'll work on it at Camelot," she said then looked back out the window.

Sophia wondered if Cundrie was thinking about her phone and how to find out where she was from. Arriving at Camelot their carriages stopped, looking out Sophia saw they had a vacant place to camp.

"Sophia, you and Kanani can wander around, but be back in one hour. The men will put up tents, I've been told Camelot is too full and we'll have to camp out here. So we will unpack and settle in after the tents are ready. Have fun," Yglais told her.

"I will, thank you," Sophia said standing up and jumping out with Kanani.

"You stick by my side, Kanani and no snatching food from anyone young lady," Sophia realized a leash was not an option here. She didn't want to do anything to draw attention herself.

Sophie, this is fun, but I'm a bit afraid of getting lost. I won't leave your side, I promise. Oh, smell all of that good food. This might be hard not to get a bite along the way.

She was amazed at all of the people, the food being put out, tents being raised and people, kids everywhere. Before she knew it, her hour was up.

"Darn, I'm going to be late we had better start back Kanani." She turned around quickly and bummed into a Knight. UMPH!

"I'm sorry, I wasn't looking where I was going." She told him gathering her composure.

"Sophia!" Exclaimed the Knight.

4

SOPHIA LOOKED up to see who knew her name and couldn't believe her eyes!

"Richard! Where's Jennie?" Sophia asked him. He was her brother-in-law that had disappeared with her sister in Egypt some time ago.

"She's back at our tent, come on she won't believe this." He said excitedly taking her hand and pulling her in the direction of his tent.

"How did you get here?" He asked looking back at Sophia again. "Hi Kanani," he said looking at her.

Hey, Richard nice seeing you. Kanani thumped her tail.

"I'd like to ask you the same thing," Sophia answered.

"Here we are, we'll exchange stories when we get Jennie's attention."

Then he stopped in front of a woman. Sophia couldn't believe it was her big sister Jennie.

"Jennie, look what I brought you home," he said.

"Now what did my handsome Knight bring me?" she asked him playfully turning around.

Jennie screamed, dropped the dish of food she was preparing and ran over hugging Sophia so tight she didn't think she could breathe. Kanani was jumping on Jennie trying to get her attention too.

"My Sophia, how did you get here? Where's Leila?" she asked her.

"Leila is home in Luxembourg and Kanani and I are here by accident." Sophia told her. "Sir Lamorak found me and I'm staying with him and his family. I've been here only a short time."

"Well it's amazing to find you here! Hi, Kanani you came with Sophia too I see. Good girl," Jennie rubbed Kanani's ears.

I like that!

"Sophia!" She heard her name and looked around. She saw Lamorak walking her way looking for her.

"I'm over here!" Sophia shouted loud enough for him to hear her over all the noise. Lamorak walked over to her.

"Hi, I'm sorry I didn't make it back but I ran into my Sister and Brother-In-Law. Let me introduce you." Sophia said taking his hand and introducing him to her family.

"Does everyone time travel in your family?" He asked shaking their hands.

"No, just my family." Sophia said laughing. She was thrilled to have her sister back into her life again.

"Tonight, is free time, let me go tell my family we ran into Sophia's family. I will be back with some food and drink then we can talk. Don't start telling any good tales without me," he turned hurrying off into the direction of their camp.

"Ok, we won't, hurry back," Sophia called after him.

"Sophia he's handsome! I think he likes you." Jennie said.

"I know but, it hasn't been that long since I lost John," she replied.

"What do you mean, you lost John?" Jennie was shocked. "What happened, did he leave you?"

"No, he was killed in a rescue mission. I'll tell you about it later. He was a good man and good to me, I miss him terribly." Sophia told her getting misty eyed.

"Oh Sophie, I'm so sorry, I didn't know," Jennie was sad for her. "I want you to know something about history regarding Lamorak. He supposedly was in love with a lady from a distant place. She left him and he was so devastated he never married and ended up getting killed looking for the Holy Grail a short time after she left him." I found this years ago when I was studying King Arthur for deposition when I went for my Doctorate. Maybe that was you! You have the ability to change all of that." Jennie said earnestly.

"Wow," Sophia was speechless. "Shh, here comes Lamorak now."

"Is Leila alright, is she here too?" Asked Jennie.

"No, she's not here. You weren't listening and yes she is alright. Leila is the reason I'm here, she insisted on going caving. She's back in Luxembourg with Susan and Kimo." Sophia answered.

Jennie was holding her hand as Lamorak walked up to them. He had a servant following him with a tray of good smelling food.

JMM ADAMS

"Is it alright to place this tray here?" Lamorak asked Jennie.

"Yes, that's fine, let me make room for it. How nice of you to feed us tonight Lamorak." Sophia told him.

"No problem at all, I get to spend the evening with my favorite Lady and learn more about her from her sister. What more could I ask for?" He was grinning from ear to ear like a little boy.

Sophia could picture him as child getting his way with everyone with that boyish grin and good humor.

"Your favorite lady?" Sophia asked.

"Did I say that? Yes, I believe I did say that my Lady!" He then bowed in front of her. "You look so lovely this evening Lady Sophia, may I be so honored as to sit next to you?"

"How could I resist your request my Lord and Knight!" She answered bowing back at him laughing.

"Well then let us all sit down and begin," Lamorak had his servant pour us some delicious red wine.

"I would like to know all about you, Lady Sophia," Lamorak took her hand and kissed it.

"I will do my best kind Sir. Jennie and I grew up moving all over the world as children. We lived with our mother in Hawaii when our father was killed in the Vietnam War. Shortly afterwards our mother died from a broken heart. Jennie and I were little so our father's grandparents took us in. Grandpa was a spy during the cold war for the United State Government. Then he worked co-op missions on special assignments. We lived in Luxembourg as children with them. That is where I was living before I came here, in grandfather's house. Now I know you are wondering what is the Viet Nam war, what is a co-op mission, I will explain that at another time."

"Please continue I am very interested." Lamorak answered.

"I ended up moving over to Maui when I turned twenty and that's where Kanani was born.

Kanani heard her name and perked up.

I love to hear stories about me.

"From there I had enough money from our father's estate to buy a small market in Lanai. John, my deceased husband, was a retired Ranger with Special Forces when I met him a long time ago. Kanani and I had a previous adventure on Maui, so the F.B.I. was called in. John did work for them too and that is how we first met. He retired and bought a small boutique hotel on Lanai to be near me. I was not aware that I had bought a hot property though. There was a map hidden in the storeroom of the market, which showed where smugglers were storing diamonds, and gold for shipment out of caves on Lanai and Molokai. Jennie and Richard's daughter Leila, Kanani, my friend Susan, and I were caught up in the middle of capturing them. My shop was torched and my yacht was totaled, then John asked me to marry him. Our friends, Susan and Kimo joined us in a double ceremony. Then we bought houses in Port Townsend, WA. Which led us into another crazy adventure. It started with the antique shop I owned. A woman came into my shop one evening towards closing. She brought me a mysterious violin from our grandfather. That violin took all of us on an adventure through France, Germany and Luxembourg. After the case was solved we ended up with Grandpa's house in Luxembourg, so Susan, Kimo, John, Kanani, and I moved there. Grandpa also left a lot of money for Jennie and myself." Sophia looked at her sister. Jennie's eyes were as round as saucers with astonishment.

"Jennie we have a lot of money in a bank for us to use, I got the house in Luxembourg and the Stradivarius." She looked at Jennie, "Can you handle me continuing?"

"Yes! Yes please go on, I'm listening. What happened to grandpa?" Jennie asked.

"Well, grandfather is in a monastery near Luxembourg and he told me briefly something we didn't know about our ancestry. Our last name is not Anderson, Jennie, it's Stradivarius!"

At that Jennie jumped up from the table knocking her plate of food onto the ground.

"Oh, I'm so sorry," she said. "Let me clean it up." Then she got up and grabbed a rag.

"No, sit," said Richard, "Sophie, please continue dear I can't wait to hear the rest of this tale!"

The servant took the rag out of Jennie's hand and cleaned up the mess as Sophia continued.

"I got a call from Leila in Egypt! She was at the Consulate and told me of her ordeal with the two of you vanishing on her. I had her flown to Luxembourg, that's where we picked her up and took her to Echternach. Then John and Kimo went back to Port Townsend to settle affairs and sell my shop, I took Leila, Susan, and Kanani to Egypt to see if we could find the two of you. We found the door you went through and Kanani and I found your notes left for Leila. I ended up here because Leila wanted to go caving in Luxembourg. We bought tickets for Egypt the following week, we were going back to go through time and look for you guys. You see, I lost John a year ago, there was never a body, but his chopper went down when he opted in a mission to go in and save some woman and children in Afghanistan. Grandpa wanted me to have something to do to take my mind off the loss of John."

"Oh, Sophia I am so sorry," said Richard grabbing her hand.

"It's ok, Richard, thank you. I'm getting over it." she said.

"How did he die on a mission if he was retired? What happened Sophia?" asked Richard.

"He was asked to re-enlist just for a special mission. The first trip in went well, and then they went back. Their helicopter was shot down and they could find no survivors. Finally, the military had the funerals with no bodies in D. C. There was a 21-gun salute using artillery and battery pieces. There were bagpipers too playing Amazing Grace. All of us widows were given medals and flags. Then an envelope was given to the other widows. I could see the look of amazement and joy when they opened them. It was money I arranged for them to have to help with expenses now that they were on their own. It was the least I could do." Sophia finished and looked around and everyone one was sitting there in disbelief.

So, after a time she continued. "Grandpa is a bit of an inventor and he gave me a phone that will work through time.

Lucky for me Susan packed the phone, because the next thing I knew I fell through a secret door with Kanani landing on top of me; that is when Lamorak found us."

"Then things started happening to me and my phone was stolen at Lamorak's, I came here with him and that is when I ran into you. That's the short version." She took a deep breath and asked, "Shouldn't we go back and get Leila? I gather the two of you want to stay in this time?"

"Yes, if we can get Leila to come back with us we'll stay," Jennie told me taking a bite of food off her new plate the servant put down in front of her.

"What a tale," Lamorak added.

"Yes, great story, Sophie," Richard said taking a drink of his wine.

"What do we do now?" Sophia asked.

5

"THAT IS something we will have to think about Sophia. In the meantime, I would like to tell you a bit about myself." Lamorak continued but Jennie interrupted him.

"I don't want to seem rude, Lamorak. Your life is very interesting; I have read all about you in history books. Sophia would love to hear about it later, but it sounds like someone has Sophie's phone, this is very dangerous. Someone could misuse this evidence and find their way into the future from Camelot. It could be dangerous."

"I don't think you are rude my Lady; I have to agree with you. I have a pretty good idea who has the phone. That will be your mission and Sophia's to find the thief while Richard and I are meeting King Arthur at the Round Table day after tomorrow. Both of you have two weeks to find out, then Richard and I will take care of the problem." Lamorak said with determination.

"Ok, I take the challenge how about you Sophie?" Jennie asked her.

"Yes, I take the challenge, but I still want the short version of your life Lamorak." She replied.

"That I will give to you sometime when we are sitting by the camp fire my Lady," he said gallantly looking at her gently.

"Ok, I'll have to accept that. So, for the next two weeks my sister and I will play detective then we will decide our fate from there, it a fair plan I can live with." Sophia told everyone, feeling pleased with the situation.

"This has been a pleasant evening, we should really be getting back Sophia, we can meet both of you after breakfast back here," Lamorak told Richard and Jennie standing up.

No, I don't want to leave Richard I like being here. Oh, ok, if you say it's ok Sophie I'll get out of my comfortable spot and follow you.

"It's been a terrific evening!" Sophia chimed in.

"I agree," said Richard standing up.

"It's been a great blessing to have found you Sophie. Thank you for the wonderful evening," my sister said wrapping her arms around her again.

"Ok girls you can be together all day tomorrow, let's go Sophia." Lamorak shook Richards hand and turned towards her.

"Ok Lamorak I'm coming with you, just a minute." Before letting go of Jennie she kissed her on the cheek, Lamorak took her hand and led her away with the servant following behind.

Sophia kept looking back until they were out of site.

"Where am I sleeping tonight, Lamorak?"

"Sophia, I have you in a small room inside the big tent, I am sleeping in the main chamber to make sure you and Kanani are safe from Cundrie and her witch craft. Plus anyone else trying to scare you away and find out your secret."

"Thank you, I can sleep peacefully tonight. The first time in a long time."

When they arrived back at Lamorak's camp, Perceval was standing by the fire, Accalon was there and they were talking. Yglais was getting up to go to sleep.

"There you two are," Yglais said, "I hope you had a nice time visiting with your sister, Lady Sophia."

"Yes I did, thank you for not minding Lamorak spending time with us tonight."

"That's fine, Lamorak can do what he wants. Good night you too." Then she walked to her tent.

"Good night Lady," Sophia said.

"Good night, Mother." Then Lamorak looked at her.

"Let me escort you and Kanani to your chambers."

"Ok, I'm beat. Come on Kanani." Kanani followed Sophia into the tent.

With that Sophia retired for the night and so did Kanani and Lamorak.

She lay down and thought of all the things that had transpired. Did she really want to go back to the future? She knew she had too at least for a while. Could she ever get back home and ever find her way back here? Sophia could stop Lamorak from getting murdered at such a young age. Sophia just couldn't solve everything in her mind; She would have to see what tomorrow would bring. With that thought she was out for the night. Kanani was laying on her feet sound asleep as well.

Sophia felt Kanani licking her and woke up. *Sophie, I hear noises outside.*

She listened, there was something going on outside. She decided they were safe where they were, rubbed Kanani's face and turned on her side going back over to sleep. The next morning Kanani woke her up early. She got up and put on a blue dress, fixed her hair and peeked out her door. Lamorak was fast asleep in the common area.

"Kanani be quiet," Sophia placed her finger over her mouth and motioned for her to listen. They tip toed past him and got outside without being heard. Sophia craved a cup of coffee; maybe her sister had some? Calling Kanani softly they made their way to her place. Jennie was already up fixing breakfast and was delighted to see them.

I had to go potty and I'm hungry, it's good to be up early. Kanani wagged her tail.

"Good morning little sister, did you sleep well?"

"Yes I did, you don't have any coffee do you?" Sophia asked hopefully.

Jennie looked at her grinning, "Do you really think I wouldn't pack everything I could for this adventure? Of course, I have coffee, let me pour you a cup."

"Really? Thank you so much," Sophia exclaimed as she picked up the warm cup and savored the smell.

"Hmmm, this is heaven. I can't remember being this happy, even with all this turmoil right now in my life."

"I know what you mean, I have to get Leila though. It was so hard not having her during the African adventure, but at least she was with you. Now she isn't with either one of us, I hope she's ok!"

"Don't worry Jennie, we'll get her soon. She loves Kimo and Susan, they are family to her just as they are to me." Sophia put an arm around Jennie and kissed her cheek.

Jennie wiped tears from her eyes and said, "Would you like some breakfast?"

"Yes please, Kanani would too, thank you," Sophia said as she handed her a plate for Kanani; then for herself.

That's good. Kanani gobbled up the scrambled eggs, licked her dish and brought it back over to Jennie placing it down in front of her.

"That's cute Kanani, but you'll have to wait for lunch." Jennie laughingly said as she carried her own plate and coffee joining Sophie around the fireplace and ate in silence.

"There you are!" Exclaimed Lamorak walking over to them. "I knew I'd find you here. Ummm, what are you drinking?"

"It's coffee, here have a taste." Sophia said as she handed him the cup.

"This is good; another modern convenience I presume?" he asked.

"Of course, keep that and I'll get another cup." Sophia stood up to get another cup.

"How about some breakfast?" Jennie asked Lamorak.

"Yes please," He said sitting down next to Sophia's chair. "Where's Richard this morning?"

"He had an errand to do. Oh, look there he is now," Jennie pointed at Richard making his way over to them.

"Good morning everyone," He walked over kissed Jennie and handed her some herbs.

"Good morning Richard," both Lamorak and Sophia said together. She looked at him and they both laughed.

"Thank you for the herbs dear," Jennie was ecstatic.

"You are very welcome, I can show you where in the woods I got them so that you and Sophie can get some more."

"Fantastic," answered Jennie.

"What are doing with them Jennie?" Sophia asked her.

"I'm using some for cooking and others for making ointments to put on Richard when he comes home cut and bleeding from his Knightly duties." She said looking at Richard and smiling.

"Well I have a lot to learn, plus we have to try and see if Cundrie took my phone and find out what she plans on doing with it." Sophia added.

"That's right," said Lamorak," it could be dangerous if she found her way to your world. If she got back to our time she would be a greater threat than Morgan Le Fay!"

"Unless they team up and go together!" Sophia exclaimed.

"Ok it's settled then. After breakfast little sister we are going to check out different merchants and keep our ears open." Jennie said.

"Deal," Sophia replied getting up to help clean the dishes.

"Wait! Richard and I are free today, we can tour Camelot together, I planned on introducing you, Sophia to Guinevere and King Arthur. We have been invited to dinner with them and I'm sure they can make space for two more, so Richard and Jennie you are invited to come along with us today."

"That's wonderful," exclaimed Jennie. "Let me put on a prettier dress, Sophie let's change your clothes too and I'll put some makeup on you. Can you Knights give us an hour?"

"We certainly can, I have some things to attend too, I will be back in a hour," said Lamorak bowing and kissing Sophia's hand. Then he turned to leave but remembered something. "Richard why don't you come with me."

"Don't mind if I do, bye ladies," he said mischievously walking off with Lamorak.

"Ok, Sophie, let's get started."

"Great idea, do you have a lot of dresses?" Sophia asked her.

"Plenty, come take a look."

With that Sophia followed Jennie into her tent and Kanani followed behind jumping on Jennie's bed. Jennie just smiled and shook her head.

"Jennie how did you end up in King Arthurs time entering through Egypt? I've been thinking about it, but can't make any sense out of it."

"There were three doors, in Egypt after we entered the main door. We tried one time period and ended up with dinosaurs chasing us, so we left. We couldn't get back out the main door so we tried another portal; this one was the Civil War age! We left that in a hurry too going through the remaining portal and hoping this one would led us to something better. It did, it was this time and we fell deeply in love with it. The only problem was that we couldn't get home to Leila. Does that help you understand a bit more?" Jeannie asked her.

"Yes, sister it does." Sophia told her turning back to find a dress she liked. Luckily, they were the same size, her sister was still slender and very pretty with her dark curly hair falling down to her waist.

6

THE MEN returned suddenly, luckily, they were dressed and ready to go. Richard popped his head into the tent.

"Jennie?" He asked.

"Yes, sweetheart we're ready, why are you guys back so soon?" Jennie asked.

"We'll explain as soon as you two are ready and come out to join us," he said, closing the tent flap and returning back to talk to Lamorak.

"Wow you are so pretty Lady Sophie," Lamorak exclaimed, as Sophia emerged from the tent in a lavender skirt falling to her ankles and a plain white top. Her sister had put Sophia's long curly dark blond hair up in a bun with strands of hair falling down around her face. Sophia felt like it made her look softer.

"Thank you kind sir," Sophia answered bowing to him with a grin.

Then Jennie walked out and Richard came over to put his arm around his pretty wife kissing her head. He was six feet tall, Jennie and Sophia weren't short, but looked short next to these two knights.

"What's the news?" Sophia wanted to know looking at both men.

"Dinner is still on, but I saw Cundrie and Morgan Le Fay talking yesterday, and found out today that they disappeared, Guinevere is gone too. The King wants to have dinner as planned, but I bet Morgan, Cundrie and Guinevere found out about you and are trying to find the opening! We need to discuss a journey back to the future and find out what they are up to. Then bring them back as soon as possible." Sir Lamorak said.

Richard agreed.

"Wow that's huge, how is King Arthur taking it?" Sophia asked.

"We'll find out tonight my dear," said Richard. With that they decided to enjoy the day anyway.

"Be a good girl and stay here Kanani. We will be back to check on you later. I love you." Sophia bent over and rubbed her dog on the head.

I don't want to stay. Can't I go to the castle too?

Sophie felt bad leaving Kanani but put her in Jennie's tent and closed the entry door.

They walked through all of the vendor tents, eating, and then took a walk through the forest gathering more herbs. After they took them back to Sophia's sisters' tent. From there they walked over and into the inner court of Camelot.

"This nothing like I imagined," Sophia said looking around.

"Me either," Jennie said with her mouth open in awe.

"Hey, how did Richard become a Knight with Arthur?" Sophia whispered to Jennie.

"We arrived some time ago and there were tryouts for being a Knight, but not a Knight of The Round Table. Richard amazed himself and me too by doing so well, they knighted him right away."

"Wow, I know John would have liked this." Sophia said wistfully.

"Sophie, John died a hero's death. He probably should never have gone on that mission, but He did something He believed in. It's been a year now that He has been gone, we can discuss this later, ok? Right now I want you to enjoy yourself little sister," Jennie chided her giving her a quick hug.

"Ok, ok, look at that!" Sophia pointed over to an ironworker making shields.

"Let's go watch him," Jennie pulled Sophia by the arm and drug her over to watch the armor being made.

Sophia looked around and saw Lamorak and Richard checking out a horse. Lamorak looked her way and smiled. She smiled and waved back then turned to watch the amazing transformation before her of metal being made into beautiful shields and knightly armor.

"Jennie, look there's a fiddler. Let's go listen to him play." Sophia told her sister as she turned to run over to the musician. He was really good, Sophia closed her eyes and listened. Sophia was a professional violinist.

She grew up playing, even learning how to build violins with her Grandfather as her teacher. She had such a love of them, Sophia could never resist violin music.

"Sophie when he's done, ask him if you can play something," Jennie urged her.

Sophia opened her eyes and looked at Jennie in horror.

"Me play the violin in King Arthur's Court?"

"Yes, Cundrie is probably already in our world and can't tell anyone about you anyway. There is nothing to lose, so have a little fun." She said nudging Sophia.

The musician finished and to Sophia's embarrassment Jennie spoke up!

"That was lovely, do you think you could let my sister play something with your violin?" Jennie asked him.

"Sure, I could use a break," he handed Sophia his violin and walked away to get something to drink before she could refuse.

"What should I play?" Sophia asked Jennie.

"I don't know, do that thing you do," She told her.

Sophia just smiled and shook her head, then started playing. She really got into it and closed her eyes as the music touched her very soul. When she looked up after the piece she played there was a huge crowd around her. They yelled, "Play more, play more!"

Sophia started another song and the owner of the violin sat down next to her picking up some Small Pipes he had laying there and started playing along. They must have played for an hour. The crowd was enjoying the entertainment; Sophia was getting thirsty but kept playing. The crowd had become so large that people drug over seats for the ones in front so the people in the back could see and listen.

Lamorak finally passed Sophia a drink of water to her great relief; She profoundly thanked him.

"Are we running late for the King?" She whispered to him.

"No, because he has the seat of honor listening." He pointed up to a balcony and King Arthur waved at them. They waved back and then Sophia turned to the bagpiper and said, "Do you know any marches?"

"Yes I do, you start one and I'll follow."

So they played until it got dark. Sophia finally handed the violin back to him thanking him for the great fun and use of his violin.

"You are welcome my Lady, let's play together again soon," He said taking a bow.

"I would enjoy that, thank you so much" Sophia said standing up as he kissed her hand.

After that Lamorak took her arm and led over to her sister and Richard, as they walked away towards the castle. Lamorak just kept smiling at Sophia, she was full of surprises.

"That was beautiful I could listen to you play all day."

"Thank you, I could play all day." She told him.

"That was incredible Sophie, I told you it would be ok." Jennie said.

"I know, thank you big sister," Sophia gave her a hug. She really meant it. She was happy for the first time in a year.

"Let's head into dinner." Lamorak said as they followed behind him into the dinner hall.

A servant met them.

"King Arthur would be honored to have you as his guests tonight, please follow me." He said.

They were placed next to King Arthur, Sophia was on one side of him with Lamorak; her sister and Richard were on the other side of him. That way they could all talk.

"It's an honor to eat with you sir," Sophia told him.

"Please call me Arthur," He said.

Then when dinner was served He got straight to the point.

"I believe, my half-sister Morgan Le Fay and your sister – in- law Cundrie, took my wife and went somewhere. I'm asking for your help. Supposedly there is some interest in where you have come from Sophia, and it has something to do with their disappearances. Either my wife left willingly or was taken." Then King Arthur waited for one of us to answer.

"I believe Cundrie has interest in Sophia's history and that She has talked to your sister, Morgan. Then the two of them convinced Guinevere to go with them on an adventure." Lamorak stated.

The King was amazed but didn't let on.

"Jennie and I need to make a trip home soon, we can look for them." Sophia told him.

"That would be good, I've spoken with Merlin and he told me to do nothing at this point in time." The King said.

"I think that's a good plan," answered Richard.

"Me too, could you please excuse me for a moment?" Sophia said standing up, "I need to use the ladies room, I will be right back. Can you point me in the right direction?" She asked.

"I'll join you," said Jennie standing up.

"Yes, go out the way you came in then go down the hall outside the dining room. It's on the right." Said Arthur.

"Ok we'll be right back."

"Do you want me to escort you?" Asked Lamorak.

"No but thank you. Jennie and I can manage ourselves." Sophia told him smiling.

They walked out of the dining room and down the hall. Before Sophia knew what happened, she was grabbed from behind!

JMM ADAMS

7

SOPHIA SCREAMED, but the hand over her mouth stopped her from making a noise. Jennie turned around and they knocked her out. Leaving her on the ground. Sophia was drug out of the Castle into the stable then roughly thrown into a carriage. The carriage took off out of the courtyard; over the moat and down the hill out of Camelot leaving a trail of dust it its wake.

"What do you want?" Sophia asked.

"We have your device and are trying to find the hole but can't. You're going to show us. There's a man on the other end and we want to meet him." Answered Morgan Le Fay.

"What do you plan on doing on the other side?" Sophia asked.

"Learning something to change history." she snorted.

Finally, they got to the area and Sophia was drug out of the carriage. She wasn't shocked, but there stood Cundrie, and Iago the page he was holding on to Guinevere, who as blindfolded and tied up. Sophia was shoved from behind and pushed towards the rock. All of a sudden Sophia saw the opening and showed them. They shoved Sophia to the ground. She hit her head and passed out. Then Cundrie, Iago, and Guinevere all went through. When Sophie woke up Lamorak was holding her hand, Jennie was wiping the dirt off of the bump on her head. Kanani was licking her face. *See, you need to stop leaving me behind. I would have protected you!*

"I'm so glad you found me," I mumbled then passed out again.

When I woke up, it was morning. I was in my cot at Camelot and everyone was standing around me. I tried to sit up. Jennie saw me struggling and ran over to help me. I had a king-sized headache. Kanani was sitting beside me with a paw draped over my chest.

"Here drink something sweetie." Jennie said bending over.

I had a drink of water then felt really hungry, but first I had to let them know what happened.

"We must let the King know that Guinevere did not leave on her own. She was tied up and blindfolded. They said some man was going to meet them. I bet that was Grandpa, he will take care of those nasty women and Guinevere will be ok. We need to go back soon though." I finished my speech and Lamorak came over and held my hand.

"Let's get you and Jennie ready to travel. How's your head?"

"It's sore, but I'll survive. We need to get home." She told him.

They spent that day getting things in order; Sophia was feeling better by the end of the day. The next morning very early before the Knight's meeting at the Round Table, Richard and Lamorak took them to the rock.

Richard and Jennie kissed then said goodbye. "I won't be gone long, and I'll be back with our daughter. So decide where we want to build our house, we have a lot of money in a bank in Switzerland. The money may not be worth anything here but we can buy stuff in our time and bring it through the portal for building our house here."

"Ok dear, be careful and come back soon." Richard replied.

With that she walked over and shook Lamorak's hand.

"Take good care of each other while were gone." She said.

"I will Lady Jennie," he said with tears in his eyes.

He turned to Sophia and kissed her hand. "I pray I see you again Lady Sophia. I have never met anyone like you."

"Thank you Lamorak, I will try to come back someday. I have never met anyone like you either. Thank you for everything you've done for me. I will miss you." She said giving him one last and an affectionate kiss on his right cheek.

Then she turned around, grabbed Jennie's hand, called Kanani, and stepped through time.

8

THEY WERE on the other side in a flash and Jennie followed Sophia out of the cave. There stood Susan, Leila and Kimo!

"I can't believe it!" Screamed Susan grabbing me, hugging me so tight I thought she was going to suffocate me. Leila jumped into her mother's arms. We all hugged, talked at once then exhausted decided to go home.

"Oh, Susan did you see anyone else come through time on your watch?" Sophia asked.

"No, Sophie, just the three of you." She was counting Kanani too.

"Oh, ok I was just wondering. I need to ask Grandpa if he knows anything."

Susan was so happy to see Sophia and Kanani. Jennie was so delighted to see Leila that the conversation died on that subject.

When they arrived home, Jennie toured the house while Sophia excused herself and soaked for a longtime in her Jacuzzi bathtub; it felt therapeutic as it relaxed her muscles and allowed her mind to drift into a la-la land.

She joined everyone for dinner before sunset feeling much more comfortable. They talked through the night taking time out to call Grandpa and planned on a trip to see him the next day. He assured everyone that Guinevere and Morgan were with him and presented no problems. Iago more or less latched onto Cundrie as soon as they got to the monastery. Neither one of them had been heard from or seen since. Sophia worried about that! Grandpa was a bit concerned as well wondering what they might be doing and are they about to interfere with the flow of time and events of the past by taking back future knowledge.

Grandpa was wondering what they might be doing and are they about to interfere with the flow of time and events of the past by taking back future knowledge.

Grandpa knew even a minor change of events in the past could have a ripple effect through time drastically effecting and changing the present.

The next morning, they arrived at the Monastery right on time and Grandpa was waiting for them in the courtyard.

"Hi Grandpa," Sophia said hugging him. She couldn't believe she was back in her world.

"Hi sweetie, I'm so happy to see you safe and sound." He said. "Hi everyone, Jennie come here my love." They had a long hug too.

"Hi Kanani," Grandpa gave her a hug too.

Kanani wagged her tail. *Nice see you again too.*

"You're a good girl for looking after Sophie." He said scratching Kanani's head.

Kanani wagged her tail. *Sophie and I are best friends, nothing will happen to her with me around.* Said Kanani in a confident manner.

After a little while we were drinking herbal tea and sitting around a large circular wooden table in the Monastery. It looked and felt a little like a particular round table in the other world.

"Well, you've stirred up quite a bit of trouble in the Middle Ages Sophie," Grandpa said looking at Sophia.

"I guess so, how it is going with them?" She asked.

"We convinced Guinevere to stay a while and learn some humility before returning. She is already believing she wants Lancelot to leave the Castle, she was horrified to find out she was the one to destroy Camelot. So, they will return home soon, perhaps a bit wiser and better and hopefully be very cautious how they go about altering even minor events so as not to change the outcome of future history."

Grandpa finished. "However, last night as you slept, we located and now have knowledge of Cundrie and Iago's whereabouts. I will keep my eyes open if I hear of any trouble and let you know."

"Fantastic, I guess it's ok to mess with history if it saves lives as long as you're careful."

"We have some things to do for Jennie and Leila's return. We'll stop in to see you before they go back Grandpa." Sophia told him. With that they said goodbye.

"Ok, see you soon my dears." Grandpa saw them off.

They arrived home after doing some errands and spent the evening talking about their visit with Grandpa.

The next morning Sophia got up early or so she thought, but Susan had a spread of food out for everyone already prepared.

"Wow, Susan this is really thoughtful of you! Thank you," Sophie said, and then gave Susan a morning hug.

"You're welcome, we have a schedule to keep today, let's get everyone up and eat so we can get going."

She then passed the plates of food around when everyone was sitting down around the table.

Kanani had already been let out and was in the kitchen eating her breakfast too.

They finished, and Sophia said, "I need to shower then I'll be ready to leave. With that she got up and went into her room with Kanani close behind. They reappeared thirty-five minutes later. Sophia was wearing a black jean skirt, blouse and Keen sandals. "Oh, it feels good to be in my own clothes again, how I missed my skirt and shoes."

Sophia had a decision to make. Did she want to stay or go back in time? It was hard to leave the luxuries of this world, but she and Kanani would have such a good time in the other world. Perhaps even make a favorable difference in history. She really had to search her soul about any decisions she was going to make.

A month went by and Sophia still had not told Jennie what she had decided, so one morning Jennie approached her.

"Little sister we need to get some money out of the bank. I need to go back, Richard is by now wondering where we are and Leila needs to get settled in her new environment."

"Yes, I agree with you. I have prayed about it and thought long and hard, I've made a decision; Jennie follow me please." She called everyone around the kitchen table.

"This has not been an easy decision, but Kanani and I are going back through time with Jennie and Leila. There is no reason for me to remain here unless anyone can think of something. Susan what do you and Kimo want to do?" Sophia asked.

"Great Sophie. We were waiting for you to make a decision. We're going where you go.

We can lockup the house here and come back from time to time." Kimo told her.

"Ok," Sophia shouted getting excited. "I need teaching supplies, we need to go to the bank and we need to go shopping!"

Sophia jumped up and grabbed her purse. Kanani went bounding over to her and Sophie snapped on her leash, grabbing the motorhome keys on the way out of the door. Everyone hurried out after her.

They piled in; their first stop was the bank. Then they bought schoolbooks, pencils and paper.

"What do you want to take with you Leila?" Sophie asked her niece.

"Lots and lots of paper and colored pencils." She shouted jumping up and down.

"Ok, off to the art supply store!"

They went to the fabric store and bought yards and yards of material. They bought anything that looked like it was from the Middle Ages.

Finally, they arrived home; it took them many trips to unload the motorhome.

They packed things in wheeled crates, so they could drag them behind themselves. Susan and Jennie ran into the sewing room and started making clothes.

Sophie grabbed Kanani's leash. "Come girl, let's go see Grandpa. Leila do you want to come with us?"

"Yes, let me tell Mom." Leila answered.

They went to see Grandpa and give him the news. He gave them two phones, so they would be able to keep in touch with him. He said that his guests would be going back in a month from now. He said he just might accompany them and go for the visit. Leila and Sophie were thrilled!

"I will always be in touch with you," Sophie told him.

"I know you will, go and live an exciting happy life Sophie. Teach those youngsters well. Leila you grow into a nice young lady, I am so proud of you. I love you all. When are you going? I want to be there to say goodbye."

"We are leaving Saturday, Grandpa can you drive us there?" Sophie asked.

"Yes, I wouldn't miss it for the world honey. I'll be there by eight a.m., is that ok?" he asked.

"Yes, that's perfect, thank you Grandpa!"

"Thank you for asking me." He got up and gave Sophie a big hug.

He laughed, "You girls get home and pack."

With that he walked them out to the car. Sophie could only wonder about his houseguests. She really doubted any of them except Guinevere would be reformed.

That night, the next day, and evening they packed.

"Sophia, are you taking your Stradivarius?" Asked Jennie.

"Yes, I am taking the Stradivarius. Why should it sit in a safe by itself when I love playing it? I could donate it to a museum, but I love playing it and it's mine." Sophia had talked herself into it.

"Ok, then let's get it packed. You might as well take the Juzek too, right?" Jennie asked her.

"Yes, absolutely!" She said going into the walk-in safe and grabbing her two violins.

Susan came in with Kimo, bringing in prepared boxes for the violins. They knew she wouldn't leave them. She assisted Kimo in getting them placed securely. He taped down the top and sides of the heavily padded box. The violins were packed for a safe journey. Jennie had left to go help Leila pack her last-minute things. Sophia didn't know how she was going to sleep that night with all of the anticipation of going back in time again. She could hardly believe it happened the first time!

9

SOPHIA WAS right; she could hardly sleep that night. She got up two times and walked through the motorhome, going over the checklists. Finally, at midnight she was so exhausted, she joined Kanani who was already in bed. Kanani put her paw around Sophie's neck and that is how they slept until Grandpa woke them up the next morning.

Grandpa arrived at six a.m., not 8 a.m. like he was supposed to.

"Good morning Papa," Sophie said opening the door and giving him a kiss. "Come in and I'll put on some coffee."

"Good morning sweetheart! Sorry I'm so early, I couldn't sleep with the fear of over sleeping and not making it here in time to take you."

"It's ok," Sophie said as she trailed off into the kitchen putting on the pot of coffee.

"Make yourself at home Grandpa, I have to go get dressed and get the others up.

"Ok, sweetheart," Grandpa said take your time. Then he sat down at the kitchen table spreading out his newspaper to read it.

At least they were all packed, Sophia thought as she went to knock on bedroom doors.

"Grandpa's here, everyone up," She shouted as She passed the bedroom doors knocking on them on the way to her own room.

Pretty soon everyone was dressed, including Sophia and they had coffee. Susan grabbed the sweet rolls and placed them out for everyone. It's just what they needed for a quick sugar high before their journey through time.

They finished, cleaned up and walked out of the house. Kimo locked the door; Sophia followed him into the motorhome. She looked back and had no regrets. She had made her decision. Finally, they were at the caves. Sophia had butterflies in her stomach and she was sure everyone else did too. Sophie was sure Kanani was the only one without a care. They got out of the motorhome and Grandpa brought out a box of phones! Well he wanted to make sure they would always stay in touch with him.

Sophia turned towards him and said, "Ok goodbye for now Grandpa, you promised to come see us soon." Sophia gave him a big hug and goodbye kiss.

"Yes, I will, goodbye for now Sophie. I will miss you, but you have enough phones to stay in touch. I'll come soon to see all of you. Perhaps after you build your homes." Grandpa hugged everyone goodbye.

"Jennie, you go first then we will send in the crates. After that Leila can go, then Kanani and myself. Kimo I think it best you come in at the end. Does that sound good to all of you?" Sophia asked.

"Yes, it's perfect," answered Jennie. Everyone agreed.

Jennie stepped through then they started sending their belongings.

It was Leila's turn, "Ok Leila go through sweetie." Sophie told her.

"I'm so excited, bye Grandpa," She said as she stepped through. She didn't hear his response.

"Kanani come here girl," Sophie grabbed her leash and they stepped through together." Sophie turned before disappearing and saw Grandpa waving goodbye, he had tears in his eyes.

Kanani and Sophie repeated their landing experience. Kanani jumped on Sophie and knocked her down again. Then she started jumping back and forth over her.

I'm so happy to be here with you, Kanani was saying in doggie talk.

Sophia looked up and was shocked to see Lamorak standing there laughing at them.

Kanani saw Lamorak and ran over to greet him too.

Richard was already arranging their belongings with Leila and Jennie.

"What were you two doing here?" Sophie asked with complete dismay.

"We have been here every day waiting for Jennie and Leila. I only had faith that I'd ever see you again." Lamorak answered.

Just then Kimo and Susan landed behind Sophie. She turned with a smile on her face and said, "Welcome my dear friends."

"Let me introduce you to Lamorak and Jennie's husband Richard."

"Nice to meet you," Lamorak said shaking Kimo's hand and bending to kiss Susan's.

"Nice to meet you too," Kimo said.

"So nice to meet such a gentleman," said Susan.

Sophie looked at Lamorak and they both laughed. Richard walked over and introduced himself too.

"Let's walk over to that pub," Lamorak said pointing across the road. "Then I can send someone to Camelot and get two carriages for everything."

"What a lovely idea," Susan said grabbing Sophie by the hand. "A real English pub! I'm so excited, come on Kimo let's go."

They walked in and sat at a long table. They ordered drinks and had a good English lunch of bread, cheese and meat. Lamorak joined them shortly after sending finding a runner to take his message to Camelot.

"It will be at two hours for the transportation, let us enjoy our time and catch up."

"Thank you Lamorak, great idea!" Sophie said adding,

"Guinevere and Morgan will be back over in about a month or so. Grandpa said they are enjoying their stay and will be changed people when they come back." She added.

"Really? It will be something to see Morgan changed! How about Cundrie and Iago?" He laughed taking a bite of bread.

"They disappeared!" Sophie exclaimed.

"Well I am sure they will stir up some trouble, I hope they are found by your Grandfather soon!" Lamorak exclaimed.

"Me too!" She replied.

"Wouldn't it be lovely to save Camelot and change history!" exclaimed Leila.

"Would it be right to change history?" Susan asked Lamorak.

"For the better it would," Lamorak answered.

"I agree," said Jennie. Everyone else just nodded thoughtfully.

An hour and a half later Leila saw the carriages approaching.

"Look they're here," Leila said running to the window.

"So, they are, that didn't take long did it Lamorak?" Sophie asked him.

"No, it didn't," he answered. "Ok everyone let me pay the tab and then let's go out and load up. Ladies use the boot if you have too, it's a long dirty trip." Then he got up to pay our bill.

"Ok, Lamorak we'll be right back," Sophie told him.

She walked to the restroom Jennie and Susan.

Jennie said, "We can't let him pay for everything, Sophie we have a lot of money."

"I know but we need to exchange it somehow. I won't let him pay for everything, I promise." She said giving her a hug.

"Ok," Jennie was satisfied.

By the time they met the men and Leila outside, the bags were loaded in one carriage. Leila had convinced the driver of the other carriage to let her sit in front with him. Jennie, Susan, Kanani and I rode inside. Kimo got on the carriage with our luggage, sitting with the driver. Not that anyone needed help, but it seemed an ok thing to do.

It happened about an hour into the trip. They were under attack by bandits! Bows and arrows started shooting at them.

10

"DUCK LEILA!" Sophie shouted out the window. "Give me your hand! Sophie put her arm out as far as she could.

Leila turned towards Sophie, but a bandit grabbed her before Sophie could get a hold of her hand. He carried her off kicking and screaming! Their driver was killed and fell beneath the wheels. Jennie was leaning out of the carriage screaming at the bandit riding off with Leila. Richard took off after him. Sophie climbed out the window and started going towards the front of the carriage. As she did this she glanced away to see Lamorak kill one bandit with a swift swipe of his sword and start chasing another. Just then her dress snagged on a low bush something as she exited out the window.

"Careful, Sophie," Susan cried getting up to help her. She lost her balance and fell from the run-away carriage. Susan was screaming at her too, as she looked out of the window Sophie had just fallen out of.

Kanani was barking, Sophie, I'm here! Don't worry I'll come for you.

Kimo's driver was wounded, but Kimo was able to stop their carriage. Lamorak saw what happened and caught up to the run-away carriage grabbing the frightened horses by their reins and bringing it to a controlled stop. Kanani jumped out the window and ran over to Sophie. She was still lying in the dirt totally shaken trying to sit up and unsnag her dress.

"Sophie," yelled Lamorak jumping off of his horse and running over to her, "are you hurt?"

"I'm just sore and my dress is ripped," she told him as he knelt beside her.

"Can you stand up?" he asked to take her hand.

"Yes, thank you." she said.

Susan and Jennie jumped out of the carriage and ran towards her too. Kanani beat them though and she was licking Sophie's face.

"Thank you, girl," Sophia said trying to get her to stop.

I told you I would save you, Kanani was saying in doggie licks.

"Where's Richard?" Sophia asked, finally succeeding in pushing her off.

"He chased the rider that grabbed Leila!" Shouted Jennie as she came up checking me out to make sure Sophia was ok.

"Here he comes now!" Jennie cried turning to run towards her husband. "Where is she?" Jennie cried.

"I almost had them and got ambushed by others hiding amongst the trees. I lost her Jennie! He cried out, h was so upset.

"What do we do?" Jennie asked Lamorak, "Do you know who they were? Where they might have gone?"

"Yes, I do, we need to get to Camelot as soon as possible, get some knights and go get hr." He said as he was helping Sophia over to the carriage.

Kimo was holding both carriages in place. "Kimo can you drive the carriage with the luggage?" Asked Lamorak.

"Yes, Lamorak I can," He said, "I think I have the hang of it."

"Good, Richard if you could grab my horse I'll drive the women."

"Ok," said Richard going over and getting Lamorak's horse.

"Everyone get in please," Lamorak was helping Sophia get seated. Kanani was sitting on Sophia's feet inside the carriage. Lamorak climbed up front and they started off.

With Kimo being a novice carriage driver, and with the wounded driver and the grief-stricken Richard, leading Lamorak's horse, they didn't move as fast as they could have.

They slowly limped into Camelot. Yglais came running out of her tent.

"Mother, get Perceval and Accalon to come here. We were attacked by the Dark Bandits, they killed Ivan and took Jennie's little girl!"

Yglais put her hands over her mouth in horror, "No, this is dreadful!" She cried as she turned and did what her son had asked of her.

Lamorak got Sophia out and into a comfortable sitting position. Women came and attended to the wounded driver.

Accalon and Perceval arrived with ten knights ready to go.

"Thank you, Mother, Men we need a plan!" Lamorak commanded.

"I want to go too," said Kimo.

"No, you are needed here Kimo. You can arrange for more tents to be put up and I need you to take care of the women." Lamorak told him, relief flooded through Susan who objected that he goes.

"Ok, I agree I can't leave my women, can I?" Where do I get more tents?"

"My mother knows, and she will assist you." Lamorak told him.

"Time is being wasted, let's ride!" Lamorak shouted. He would formulate a plan as they rode.

The knights cheered, and Sophia cringed.

11

"BE CAREFUL and come back alive," Sophia pleaded.

"We will My Lady, don't worry. We have the greatest knights around. Will you be ok?" he asked.

"Yes, just hurry back," she told him.

"Ok goodbye then!" Lamorak called as he charged off in front of the knights.

"Sophie I'm so scared," said Jennie grabbing her hand.

"Me too," Sophia cried. "This is tragic."

"Sophie and Jennie, I'm going to help Kimo get the tents set up, then I will come back and help around here."

"Thank you, Susan," Sophia told her. As Susan left to help Kimo Yglais approached Sophia.

"Let's look at you my dear," Yglais said. "Let's get you out of these filthy clothes and see what damage has been done. You're going to be very sore later on, I just want to make sure nothing is broken."

"Thank you, Jennie can you come with us?" Sophia asked her sister.

"Yes, sweetie let's go," Jennie said.

Then they took her into the tent and Sophia got cleaned up. She had a very bruised leg and back with some scratches, but nothing seemed to be broken.

Kanani was right behind Sophia. I'm here with you. Look I can make you feel better. Kanani was rubbing up against Sophia whining.

"Kanani I don't mean to ignore you. Of course, you can come with us girl." Sophia seemed to read her dog's mind.

12

LAMORAK LED the knights deep into the forest, and then suddenly put up his hand for complete stillness and quiet. They heard horses riding through the forest. "Get your arrows ready," he whispered.

He positioned everyone off the main path on two sides. Just within the trees. They came closer and closer; he put down his arm to signal the attack. The battle was bloody; many of the Dark Bandits were killed.

"Where is the child?" Lamorak commanded talking to a fallen Bandit with his sword pointed at his chest. "I will spare your life if you tell me where she is!"

"The child is tied up a mile from here in a tree," he spat out.

"Show me!" Commanded Lamorak as he roughly jerked the captive to his feet.

Lamorak followed the man while leading his horse. Richard and a few knights fell behind Lamorak while the others were waiting for their return on the main road.

"Daddy!" Screamed Leila when she saw them coming. "I'm up here."

"I see you baby, were coming." Richard shouted back hurrying as fast as he could.

They got there, and Richard climbed the rope ladder to cut her loose.

"Oh Daddy," she sobbed, "I was so scared!"

"I know honey, but you're alright now." He hugged his daughter and brought her down, then placed her in front of him on his saddle.

Lamorak pushed the bandit and told him to go away. He could have killed him, and any other man would have, but to Lamorak that seemed immoral and he wasn't going to lose his soul.

With that they caught up with the other knights and returned to Camelot.

13

KIMO HAD more tents set up, while Susan made the beds, then put away their clothes. Most their luggage was put away, except for the school supplies by the time the knights came back to camp. Richard rode into camp with Leila; Jennie ran over and grabbed her off the saddle. She hugged her so tight it hurt, but Leila didn't care. She was home with her family again.

Sophia was starting to be in terrible pain from her fall off the carriage. She wished she had a painkiller; Lamorak came over to see how she was doing. Sophia asked him to help her into her tent to lie down.

"Can you come back for me in an hour?" she asked him.

"Yes, do you want me to stay?"

"No, I need to try and get ahold of my Grandpa but thank you for asking."

"You are welcome, I'll check back soon." he said, then turned around and left.

Sophia reached into her pack and got out her phone. She turned it on while Kanani jumped up on her bed waiting to snuggle.

I'm here with you Sophie, I love you.

"Are you ok girl?" Sophia asked her, Kanani wagged her tail and Sophia rubbed her head. It was such a comfort to have her.

Picking up the phone se dialed Grandpa's number. He answered on the first ring.

"Hi Sophie, you made it my dear! I am so pleased to hear from you." Grandpa wouldn't let Sophia get a word in.

Finally, she got to speak. "Grandpa we made it, but there was an incident soon after we returned; then she relayed the story."

"Well I'm glad Leila was unhurt, but what about you dear, do you need to come home and get checked out at the hospital?" he sounded concerned.

"I think I will be ok Grandpa, I will go back if I need too, but it will just take time for these bruises to heal. At least I didn't hit my head, so I know I will be fine." she reassured him. The hour went by quickly, because Lamorak came into Sophia's tent before she was done talking to Grandpa on the phone.

"I will call you tomorrow Grandpa, I have to go. I love you," she told him.

"Goodbye dear, I love you too." With that they disconnected.

"I brought you some dinner, then why don't you try to rest Sophia. We can get more done tomorrow if you aren't so sore and tired." He handed her a plate of food and set a dish down for Kanani too.

Oh, thank you Lamorak, you are a pretty good host, Kanani was thinking as she gobbled her dinner.

"Thank you, I'm forever grateful," Sophia was saying as she took the dish of food from him. He sat down next to her and they talked until she finished. Then he took Kanani out for potty.

When he came back with her they said good night. Sophia got up and brushed her teeth then went to bed, with Kanani sleeping next to her.

Well as long as I'm with you Sophie I don't care if we don't have our comfy bed back home. Kanani was thinking as she fell asleep.

Sophia dreamed of bandits and of John. Could she go back in time and find him before he gets killed? Was that possible? Should she just let it go and pursue saving Lamorak and educating children in this century? Tomorrow would bring new adventures.

14

A FEW MONTHS had gone by, Sophia's bruises were healed and the builders they had hired were hard at work building their homes. They decided to build them in Camelot, because Sophia wanted to open a school closer to where more children lived. Also, it was much safer being in Camelot than where Lamorak's castle was located. King Arthur sent out several knights on a quest, one that Lamorak was supposed to be on, but didn't go because of Sophia. It was a good thing, because those knights were ambushed and brutally killed. They were on a quest to save the last of the white dragons. Rival knights from the north, looking to kill the dragons, ambushed and killed all of the King's knights that went on the mission.

It was late one afternoon that Sophia noticed again how Kanani kept disappearing at the same time of day. This was a dog that would never leave her side. Today, Sophia excused herself from her sister when she saw Kanani taking off again. They were watching over the builders, getting minor details fixed.

Too Sophia's amazement she saw Merlin the Wizard! Should she be worried? *That sneaky little dog, what was she up to without me?*

Sophia followed them through the market; people threw Kanani tidbits of food. Sophia was getting upset; she didn't like Kanani to go off of her diet like that. She had to change things soon.

Next, they went through the cemetery gate by the side of the castle. She followed them through and watched them go around to the back of the castle and go through a door. Merlin unlocked it and let Kanani in, then himself.

What was this about? Should se wait? She decided to hide behind a headstone and see what would happen next. Sophia made herself as comfortable as possible. It was getting later in the afternoon and her stomach was growling, she was hungry. It was time to go back and make dinner, but she decided to wait ten more minutes. Finally, he door opened and Kanani came out running right past Sophia, high tailing it back home without noticing her.

Pant pant, *I'd better hurry, Sophia will be looking for me.* Kanani sprinted through the market not even stopping to beg.

Merlin left shortly after and presumably went back to his place. Sophia hesitantly went over to the door and turned the knob. It was a heavy door, Merlin forgot to lock it, she pulled it open. Sophia walked into the dark cold hall, she couldn't see in front of her so she put her hand against the wall. She felt her way down the winding hallway and then all of a sudden someone spoke to her! She stifled a scream and held her breath. She wanted to run!

15

"WHO GOES there?" The voice said.

Sophia froze, terrified.

"I know you're there, say something!" The voice said again getting agitated.

"Um, Sophie."

"Well, who is Sophie?" The voice asked.

"Kanani's human," she answered shakily.

"Oh, I like Kanani. Do you know Merlin?" The voice continued the conversation. It sounded like a young voice.

"Yes, not well but I saw him. I noticed Kanani missing every day for a while and today followed her to see what she was up too. Who are you," Sophia asked?

"My name is Gunther, I'm a friendly dragon." he replied.

"A DRAGON?" Sophia shouted! She didn't mean to shout, but a dragon? She didn't believe in dragons.

"I won't hurt you!" he whined back at her.

Sophia grabbed the wall tighter and inched forward two more steps. She peaked around the corner. She was amazed; it was the most beautiful place she had ever seen. It must have been the length of the whole castle! There were lights, windows, trees, grass, and a cave for Gunther. There was everything here to make him feel like he was living outside. Then she laid her eyes on

Gunther! He was the most beautiful creature she had ever-laid eyes on!

"What are you doing in King Arthur's dungeon?" she asked him.

He answered saying, "Men are killing all of the white dragons. There was an awful battle, my parents were killed and King Arthur saved me. I was a baby and he brought me here to hide me. There are more of us that need saving. Merlin comes to talk to me and feed me daily. I dream of being outside and being able to go wherever I want to go. Merlin agrees something must be done with me soon."

"Well, let me see what I can find out. Is there anything I can bring you? "

"Yes, will you come back again with Kanani to talk to me?" Asked the dragon.

"Yes, but I must go for now, I will be back tomorrow."

"Ok, good night," Gunther told her.

"Good night, Gunther," she told him, then turned around and made her way back down the hallway and outside. She closed the door and sat down in disbelieving awe. Sophia looked around. Did she just talk to a dragon? She had to go find Lamorak.

16

SOPHIA RAN back to their homes being built, found Kanani and stared at her. She jumped on Sophia and gave her tons of kisses.

"I know what you've been doing," Sophia told her.

All Sophia heard was woof, but Kanani was really saying. *What do you mean? I'm a good girl.* She cocked her head looking at Sophia like a little innocent dog.

"Hmm, let's get my sister if she's still here, go back to camp and start dinner. I need to find Lamorak," Sophia told her.

She looked around; Jennie had already gone back to camp so Kanani and Sophie decided to see what had been done that day. The homes were almost complete. She was getting so excited!

They got back to the camp and everyone wanted to know where they had been. So, sitting around the table at dinner that evening she confided in her sister, Leila, Richard, Susan, Kimo, and Lamorak, who had made it back from working with King Arthur that day.

"Did you know anything about this Lamorak?" she asked him

Yes, I knew King Arthur had saved a dragon, but never had a clue he was in the bottom part of the castle! It doesn't seem like a good place to live for a dragon, does it?" He asked looking at her with a questionable expression.

"No, it doesn't, and he said that there were more that needed saving, which we know already." she replied quickly.

"Yes, well I will speak to Merlin tomorrow. Are you and Kanani up for a quest, Sophie?" He asked her.

She looked at him with shock, "What kind of quest?" she asked him with suspicion. "The kind where we take Gunther and go find his relatives, then bring them back here. There are caves back behind where you're building your homes. We could make a nice place for them back there and then they could help keep a watch over Camelot!" he exclaimed.

"Well, that's a grand plan, let me think about it tonight and let's see what Merlin has cooked up before we decide, ok?" she answered.

"Ok, sounds logical," he said.

"I want to go too!" Piped in Leila.

"Oh no you won't do that!" Said Jennie to her daughter.

"Mommmm, pleassssseeeee?" Pleaded Leila.

Before Jennie could answer Sophie said, "Leila, let's see what the plans are and not worry about it tonight, deal?"

"Ok, but you had better not leave me behind." she grumbled.

Susan just laughed as she got up to clean the dishes.

Sophia got up, gave Leila a hug and helped Susan; then they joined the others by the campfire singing their evening away.

The next morning, Jennie, Leila, Susan, Kimo and Yglais left to go check on the progress of the builders. Richard, Lamorak and Sophia met with Merlin in his house. Then they had a meeting with King Arthur and it was decided that a quest was to begin. They would leave as soon as they could get everything together. Sir Lamorak, Sir Perceval, Sir Accalon, Sir Degore, Sir Alymere, Sir Bedivere, Sir Lancelot, Merlin, Kanani, and Sophia would be in the party. Gunther was consulted, and he was getting very excited about being with them. They drew up a plan that if they were attacked, Kanani and Sophia were to get on Gunther and he would take them to safety.

At dinner that night Sophia was so thrilled she could hardly eat. Lamorak and Sophia had filled the others in on their meetings that day. Leila wanted to go so badly, but her mother and Sophie told her it was far too dangerous, and she needed to remain at home. Sophie assured her that she would have plenty of dragons to play with if they were successful. That satisfied her somewhat. Sophie was worried about taking Kanani, but there was no way she would stay here without her. She knew she would try and find her and that would be far more dangerous for her. Sophia debated on taking one of her violins; she had never been without one since the age of four. It would be a shame for her to lose the Stradivarius and she loved her Juzek just as much. So, she decided perhaps this would be the first time she would be without a violin.

Yes, I am leaving it here, she told herself.

The morning of their departure saw all of Camelot out cheering or their success. They were on a quest to rescue the remaining white dragons in the world! They would be up against other kingdoms if any rivaling knights crossed their path. They would be traveling far far away to a distant land. They would have Merlin report to King Arthur on their progress. No one knew how long they would be gone.

Gunther was having so much fun; he practiced flying every day to get ready for this quest, so he was in fine form by the time they departed.

Kanani was placed on a horse with Sophie; all of the knights were ahead of them. *I'm so excited! Sophie always does such fun things!* Gunther and Merlin were riding beside them. Jennie was crying, and then ran over trying to stop Sophia by waving her hands.

Sophia stopped her horse and when Jennie reached her she said, "Don't forget your phone so you can call when the quest is finished Sophie," and then she handed Sophie the phone.

"Thank you, very much big sister," she said as she grabbed the phone and they continued on their way.

Sophia saw Susan running over to Jennie putting her arm around her to give reassurance. Kimo was waving goodbye too. Sophie and Kanani then caught up with Merlin.

They traveled north all day and finally stopped to set up camp many hours later before dusk that night.

"Lamorak, how far have we come and where do you think we are?" Sophia asked him.

"We have come about 1000 paces and we have many to reach Northern Scotland. We might be in for some action with rivalry knights when we get farther north." he answered. "Here's a copy of our route in case we get separated." Sophia took the map and tucked it into her pocket.

"Thank you Lamorak."

"Gunther, do you feel good about this trip?" Sophia asked the dragon.

"Yes, I am very excited. I wish I could fly ahead and see what is there." He said.

"That would be too dangerous Gunther, that is why you must stay with us." Lamorak reminded him.

"I know," answered Gunther scratching his front paw on the ground to make a comfy bed to sleep in as the group began to settle in for the night.

They traveled two more weeks with no incidents, and then Merlin decided to let King Arthur know their whereabouts. He took out one of his doves out of his bag and tied a note on to his leg and let him go.

The next morning, they packed up and started on their way. It happened around noon when they were getting close to a forest. They walked into an ambush! Arrows flew over their heads! Sophia's horse reared up and she fell off with Kanani. Her phone slipped out of her skirt pocket. She tried to grab it, but in all the confusion missed. Lamorak jumped was off his horse grabbing her and pulling her towards Gunther. He called Gunther to come get Sophia and Kanani.

17

"GUNTHER COME here!" he yelled at the dragon.

"Hurry, take Sophia and Kanani," Lamorak told him.

Gunther put his head down and Lamorak shoved Sophia onto the big dragon, and then handed Kanani to her. Merlin jumped on too. As soon as they were on him Lamorak told him to fly away. Then he grabbed his sword, and turned to fight. Sophia held on and looked down at the battle below. Gunther was flying fast and high so they could only see specks on the ground. She was frightened that Lamorak would get killed; that they would be lost. Merlin was sitting behind her on Gunther. That at least gave her some comfort!

I'm here with you Sophie, I love you. Slurp Slurp. Kanani kissed Sophia.

"Thank you, girl. I love you too." Sophie told her.

"I should go back and help fight," said Gunther.

"No," said Merlin, "we are here to protect you."

"Merlin, couldn't he put us somewhere and go back and fight?" Sophie pleaded.

"No, the orders were for Gunther to take off with us, Sophia. Gunther why don't you land over there." Merlin was pointing to point high small clearing deep in the forest.

Gunther turned towards the forest and slowly guided down between the trees. He let them off. Sophia looked around. It was a gorgeous jungle. However, she was visibly shaken. With a sword in her hand she sat upon a tree trunk. Kanani came over and put her head on Sophie's lap giving her comfort. Gunther put his paw beside Sophie and stared into her face. Merlin climbed a tree and looked behind them to see if anyone was coming their way. It was very peaceful. Would the others find them? Where they still alive?

18

LAMORAK WAS glad that Sophie and Kanani were safe; he went into battle with rival knight, fighting to the death. Perceval was swinging his sword and wounding his attacker. Lamorak swung his sword and killed him. Then they turned around and fought more knights coming towards them. It was a bloody battle, Lamorak was tired and his sword was growing, he looked around. The attacking knights had called a retreat and they fled taking their dead. To his sorrow, he saw that Sir Degore, Sir Alymere, and Sir Bedivere, were lying on the ground. He went over and checked, they were gone. Sir Lancelot was wounded, but able to ride, so it only left Sir Perceval, Sir Accalon, and Lamorak to bury the dead. "That was Gawain's men that attacked us, did Gawain survive?" Lamorak asked Perceval and Accalon.

"I don't know, when are they going to let this feud go? We didn't kill his father!" Yelled Perceval angrily to the fleeing rival knights.

"I don't know. Lancelot, are you ok to move forward?" asked Lamorak.

"Yes, we have some horses that didn't run off. We need to get them and ride as far as we can tonight." Lancelot answered.

With that they picked Lancelot up and mounted the horses; the doves had all flown out of the Merlin's bag and were gone.

Lamorak was hoping when they all arrived in Camelot together with no message tied to them, perhaps King Arthur would know what happened and send more men to help them. They couldn't worry about that now, they needed to find Sophia and Gunther.

Where did that dragon take them? Lamorak asked himself.

19

WHEN MERLIN came down from the tree, he caught some rabbits with his magic and that is how Sophia saw him approaching. Gunther made a fire with one hot breath to keep them warm, while Sophia and Kanani gathered some herbs.

"Hi Merlin, any sign of them?" she pleaded.

"No, my dear there isn't. We can't stay out here in the open; I saw a waterfall and lake not far from here. We need to go that way, pointing towards the northwest, perhaps there will be a cave we can occupy. Let's put out this fire and start walking towards it."

"Ok, I agree, Merlin." Sophia said stomping out the fire to follow him.

A boar charged at them from the woods! Gunther killed him with his dragon fire. It was amazing; Gunther was shocked too. He had never breathed fire before! Now they had enough food for a big dinner, dragons can sure eat a lot. They drug the bore behind them and approached the waterfall. Kanani was so happy to see water she jumped in and swam around. *This is so much fun!*

"Look, there's a cave behind the waterfall," Merlin pointed out. "Stay here, I will see if it's empty."

"Ok," Sophia stayed where she was, watching Kanani swim. She was having a great time splashing around. Sophia laughed, in spit their situation they could still have some fun.

"The cave's empty," said Merlin, "let's make a fire at the opening."

"Oh, this is nice," Sophia said walking behind the waterfall. Kanani came running up shaking herself all over them.

Oh joy. Thanks, Kanani, just what I needed. She thought sarcastically. The opening and cave were big enough for Gunther too. They ate dinner and then sat around the fire talking about the day. Hoping that the knights were ok and coming to find them soon.

20

CASEY LANE rolled out of bed and just about hit the floor hard. The phone was ringing; it was the middle of the night and Jackie Lee, her German Shepherd Dog, had taken over her whole queen bed, covers and all. She groped for the phone.

"Casey Lane and Jackie Lee GSD Detective Agency," She mumbled into the phone.

"Yes! Yes, hello, my name is Father Anderson, I want to hire you and your dog to go find my granddaughter, she's missing. I know where she is; but it's awkward to explain over the phone. Can you fly to Luxembourg and meet me, and then I can explain?"

Casey Lane turned on the light and looked at the clock, it was five a.m. time to get up soon anyway. She was listening with interest now. Jackie Lee was snoring and lying on his back. Really, he had to get up soon too.

"Well, we can fly to Luxembourg and meet you, but I can't promise we'll accept the assignment." She told him.

"I will have tickets for you at Sea Tac, can you go tonight?"

Whew, tonight she thought!

"Umm, we just finished a big assignment, so we could catch a flight out tonight. Will you pick us up?" She asked him.

"Yes, I will be there to get you." he replied.

"Ok, let me call and make a reservation." she told him.

"It's already done; you leave at 8 P.M. tonight on Lufthansa. Have a safe flight and thank you." He replied then hung up.

Casey looked at the dead phone in her hand. What was this all about? She put the phone down thinking about all she had to do.

"Jackie Lee, up and at'em kid," she said leaning over the bed giving him morning rubs.

"Arrrr," He mumbled smiling at her with his big white teeth. *Is it really morning?*

"You're a character Jackie Lee, let's go." She said with a smirk.

They hit South Beach for a bit of exercise and by noon were home and packed. Casey Lane notified her boyfriend of sorts that they would be out of town, to please keep an eye on her house. He was a State Trooper, so she wasn't sure where he was right now. He wouldn't be happy she had left without saying goodbye, so that's why she at least left him a message. Jackie Lee was wearing his doggie armor suit, Casey Lane had her suitcase packed very lightly and they caught the ferry from Friday Harbor, Washington, that's where Jackie and Casey lived, to drive down to the airport in Seattle and wait for their flight.

The airline was very accommodating to Jackie Lee; he got a seat next to Casey Lane in first class. It was a bit of a fiasco getting through security with Jackie Lee's body armor.

"It was very nice of Mr. Anderson or Father Anderson to pay for our fare overseas." Casey said to Jackie Lee.

It was very nice of him. Jackie Lee thought.

Everyone one on the flight thought Jackie Lee was so adorable; of course, Casey did too.

They were greeted at the airport without a wait and driven to a beautiful estate. Father Anderson told Casey this was Sophia's house, used to be his until he joined a monastery.

They walked in; Casey Lane was stunned at the very beauty of the place. The off-white marble floors in the entryway, a huge chandelier hanging overhead, wainscoted walls, polished wooded floors, she shook her head in amazement. There seemed to be many rooms however they were shown into the kitchen.

"This is the house you and Jackie Lee can stay in tonight, I have prepared a dinner for us and thought we could talk about my proposal during that time. Then if you agree, I will take you to the destination tomorrow, does that sound good to you?" Asked Father Anderson.

"Yes, yes, could I just take Jackie Lee out for a quick walk?" Casey Lane asked him.

"Perfect idea, then I will have the food ready when you get back. What does Jackie Lee eat?" Asked Father Anderson.

"I have his food packed in dry ice, thank you for reminding me. I need to get it in the fridge right away. Then we'll go out Jackie Lee," she looked at her dog; he was giving her big eyes when she mentioned his food.

Did you say food? He got up and wagged his tail, then pawed her.

"In a minute, while I get your food unpacked, go get your leash!" She told him. With that he trotted off to the front door and came back with the leash in his mouth. He remembered she had left it at the front door as soon as they entered the house.

Everything was accomplished, Jackie Lee had his walk and dinner; he was now lying down at her feet. They were eating, and Casey Lane was listening in disbelief at the tale of Sophie and Kanani.

"Well, what do you think? Would you go and take a look, then get back to me? My older granddaughter, Jennie, is very worried about them. I think, but don't know for sure if my great granddaughter went with Sophia and Kanani as well as Lamorak and Merlin. Something must have happened, or we would have heard from them by now. They have been gone nine weeks!" He looked very worried indeed.

"I will go over and meet with Jennie, then see if I can be of any help. I don't know much about finding dragons, I don't even believe they ever really existed and I don't believe I can go back in time. However, if this is true, Jackie Lee needs to stay here with you until I return. I don't feel comfortable with him going through time. Is that a deal?" she asked.

Getting up to shake her hand Father Anderson said, "That's a deal, Jackie Lee will have to come back to the monastery with me and stay there until you return. Just tell me how to care for him and feed him. I'll be anxious to hear your report. I'll call Jennie now, so she can meet you tomorrow when you arrive." He got up and walked into another room.

Casey Lane scratched her dog on the head, "I don't believe any of this Jackie Lee, but he seems like a sane person. You be a really good boy, ok?" She didn't expect an answer, but he gave her a high five.

I'll be seeing you soon, right? Just come back for me. Man was she going to miss him.

"Ok, it's all set for tomorrow. We will leave here around seven a.m. if that's ok with you?" He asked.

"Yes, that's fine. Where should Jackie Lee and I sleep tonight? I'd like a shower too and I need to repack a smaller bag to take with me." She added.

"Follow me, you can have this guest room, there's a tub and shower attached to the room and fresh towels." He said as Casey Lane got up from the table and followed him to a room off the kitchen.

"Thank you and good night," she said as he walked away.

"Thank you too," he said turning around to look at her, "good night."

With that they were alone. She didn't know what she was getting herself into and why would anyone leave this beautiful house to go to the middle ages? Strange! She needed sleep. Pretty soon Jackie Lee was snoring away next to her. If she hadn't been so tired she would not have fallen asleep so fast herself.

Morning came all too fast, Jackie Lee was left in the car or no one could have stopped him from coming with her on her journey. She cried when they hugged goodbye.

She was talking to Father Anderson and before she knew it, she had stepped through an opening. Darkness bounded all around her, she was all alone; it went by very fast, then she landed hard on the ground. She looked around and saw a carriage coming her way.

I sure hope they're coming for me, she said to herself. *Unbelievable, the old man was telling me the truth!*

The carriage stopped in front of Casey Lane. Jennie jumped out of the door.

"Hi, I'm Jennie, you must be Casey Lane. Where's Jackie Lee?" Jennie stuck out her hand to shake Casey's and looked around for Jackie.

"Hi, yes I'm Casey and I left Jackie with your grandpa. I was worried about him coming through time."

"Well, Kanani has come through many times and it hasn't bothered her a bit. Kanani is a German Shepherd too. So, he would've been ok, but Grandpa will take good care of him. He loves German Shepherds. Come on, let's grab your bag and go back to Camelot." Jennie then grabbed Casey's little bag and they jumped into the carriage.

"I'm in shock. Did I really go through time?" Asked Casey.

"Yes, you did, I know it's a bit far-fetched, but it really happened. Welcome to our new world Casey. Thank you for coming. Let me catch you up on what has happened so far. By the time the carriage arrived in Camelot, Casey was up to speed on the story of Kanani, Sophia, and Gunther. She was introduced to

Richard, Susan and Kimo. Then that night they sat around the campfire going over their plans. King Arthur was going with more of his knights, Richard, Jennie and yes, Leila were going too. In fact, they were taking a lot of people with them. They had their carriages loaded up the next day, Casey met King Arthur and they dressed up Jennie, Casey, and Leila in armor for women.

"You look fabulous!" Said Jennie to Casey.

"So do you!" Said Casey. "You think these will be comfortable for the long trip? I guess they want to make sure we're protected. Not exactly 'lightweight' for traveling." She laughed.

"I think they'll be fine. Wait until Richard sees how stylish I am in this armor!" Jennie laughed too.

21

YGLAIS AND AFAWEN, the maid, waved goodbye to all of them as they took off for Scotland, looking for the lost party.

There were so many of them that it looked like all of Camelot had left. Yglais was sad to see them all depart, but she prayed her sons would be found alive. Some of King Arthur's Knights had stayed behind, and Yglais was going to be busy making sure the homes were finished and the caves prepared in hopes of many dragons returning with them.

JMM ADAMS

22

'ARE YOU thinking what I am Jackie Lee?" Grandpa asked Jackie Lee when they had finished a big dinner and were sitting in front of the fireplace.

WOOF! Said Jackie Lee giving Grandpa a high five. *I say we go get her!*

"Well, I feel the same way. Let's go pack, we're going to go find them tomorrow boy!" With that Grandpa jumped up and Jackie Lee took off after him. Yahoo!

He knocked on a door.

"Yes? Who is it please?"

"It's Father Anderson, can you open up Morgan Le Fay?"

The door cracked open.

"We need to talk," she opened the door and Grandpa told her what was transpiring in Camelot. She agreed they were needed back home.

"Let's go talk to Guinevere," Grandpa said as he stood up to go out of the door. The three of them went over to Guinevere's door and knocked.

"Open up, we need to talk to you about something important," Morgan sniffled as she talked.

"What's going on?" Asked Guinevere as she let them into her room.

They told her. She agreed. So, everyone departed to their own rooms and packed that evening. In the morning they were going to Camelot. The party shouldn't be too far ahead of them.

23

GUNTHER DECIDED to take a swim. He jumped into the pool of water under the waterfalls. Kanani jumped in after and swam circles around Gunther as he splashed in the water. Sophia was laughing so hard she doubled over holding her stomach. This at least was some relief from the stress of waiting for the rest of their team to arrive. This went on for a while then Sophia saw Merlin come walking back from his daily task to the watchtower. Every day Merlin walked back to the same place Gunther took them when fleeing from the enemy. He climbed that same tree and watched to see if he could see any signs of Lamorak and the others. It was no different today; he looked so disheartened it made Sophie feel bad.

"Hi Merlin, still no sign of anyone?"

"No Sophia, nothing. I think we should talk about leaving tomorrow and having Gunther fly us to our destination. It will take a lot longer for anyone to ride a horse or walk there, so we will have plenty of time to look for Gunther's family. What do you think?" Merlin asked her.

"I think it's a good idea, Merlin. Maybe we just missed them because they didn't come this way through the woods."

"True, so we need to depart in the morning. It looks like Gunther and Kanani are having a lot of fun. They deserve it."

"I agree Merlin. Come sit next to me and talk. We can start dinner soon."

"Alright." With that Merlin sat down next to her so they could plan their next move.

In the morning they gathered their supplies and scrambled onto Gunther.

"Gunther let's fly back a bit and over the road to see if we can find anyone in our group." Said Merlin.

"Ok, I can do that, is everyone ready?" asked Gunther.

"Yes, Kanani and I are all ready, Merlin is aboard too, so lets go Gunther." Sophia said.

"Ready for takeoff, Gunther is going," he said.

He flew them back to the edge of the forest; they searched the ground under them and saw no one. Then he flew over the dirt road winding through the thick forest for a long time and still they saw nothing. Sophia was so disappointed but knew in her heart they had to go on. She had lost her phone, the only communication with the outside world. They were truly on their own in a century from long ago.

Gunther then turned and flew over the forest so they would be protected from anyone seeking to harm them, and headed for Scotland. That night they got into what is now known as Ayr; on the western border of Scotland; along the shore of the Firth of Clyde. It was beautiful! They found a cave to sleep in acing the water. Merlin got them some food and they camped that night with no fire. They didn't want to attract any attention to themselves.

Sophia was so happy they had not encountered any enemies. In the early morning hours, barely twilight, they heard noises.

"Shh," said Merlin as he got up and crept out towards the cave entrance. He motioned for Sophia to come to him. She groggily got up and looked out.

There were Trolls walking through the area!

24

SOPHIA CREPT back and woke Gunther, she told him what was happening. He was scared, but let Kanani and her get on him, Merlin got on the back end of Gunther. The brave dragon crept out of the cave, a Troll saw them and started throwing rocks at them, it made some loud noises and then the Troll's friends came running up behind him to attack them too! Merlin grabbed his wand from his robe, pointed it at the Troll in front, said something, and he turned to stone! Then he did the same to the next one. The rest of the Trolls turned and ran in terror!

"Merlin will they stay that way?" Sophia asked him.

"For eternity I hope! We need to get far from here as quickly as possible before anything else happens!" He explained. It was just turning daylight as they left on their journey.

~~~~~~

"Look up there!" Screamed Perceval as he pointed at the white dragon in the sky ahead of them.

"That's Gunther with Sophie, Kanani and Merlin!" Shouted Lamorak.

All the men yelled at the Dragon and sped up on their tired horses. It was to no avail; they were too far behind them and could not be heard. At least they knew they were alive and well. Now only if they could make better time.

~~~~~~

25

GUNTHER FLEW all day until Sophia insisted he find a safe place to land and take a break. So, he found a place to land in the town of Arbroath on the east border of Scotland about 150 miles northeast of Ayr. They landed on the beach, Merlin went to find some water and Gunther jumped with Kanani into the ocean to get refreshed. Sophia walked around; it was a sandy beach, with magnificent sandstone cliffs stretching out all around them. Sophia kicked off her shoes and walked on the sandy beach letting the waves wash over her feet. She smelled the clean sea air and grabbed a stick, then threw it for Kanani to fetch.

Yipppee! I love chasing sticks, I love water!

Gunther was happy too! How she loved that dragon. Merlin came back with good news, not far from where they were a small stream flowed with fresh drinking water. They followed him there and everyone got a large drink of water. Sophia pulled out some food that they still had and they had a lite snack. Gunther caught a fish and ate that.

"Do you feel like traveling anymore today Gunther or should we stop here for the night?" Sophia asked the dragon.

"I'm a bit tired, could we stay here tonight?" Gunther pleaded.

"Merlin, what do you think?" Sophia asked.

"Let's stay here for the night, Sophia. Then we can have a fresh start in the morning, we've travelled a great distance today and I know we're tired."

"I agree, it's settled then. Let's set up a little camp site for the night." Sophia said, and then got up to start setting up camp.

"I can catch more fish," said Gunther.

"Good, Merlin can you find some herbs for us eat or do you want wood duty?" she asked.

"You go get the herbs Sophia and I will do the fire." said Merlin.

"That's a deal, Kanani you can come with me. I'll meet all of you back here soon." With that Kanani and Sophia took off looking for herbs.

~~~~~

Lamorak, Perceval, Accalon and Lancelot had been riding their horses all day. They were exhausted and Lamorak was sick with worry for Gunther, Sophia, Kanani and Merlin. Merlin could at least take care of them a bit, but they were so far ahead and would get to Gunther's homeland weeks before any of them could get there. They had been lucky to not run into any more rival knights. Lamorak didn't know how long that luck would run for them. They stopped and camped about the same time Gunther, Sophia, Kanani and Merlin did.

~~~~~

Grandpa, Jackie Lee, Guinevere, and Morgan went through time. Jackie Lee was jumping up and down running all around. Guinevere was laughing, it was so good to be back, and Jackie Lee was way too funny.

"Ok, what do we do now? There is no transportation." Grandpa said.

"Well, Lamorak's Castle is a short walk from here. We can make it there and hopefully get some horses or a carriage to Camelot." Said Guinevere.

"We need to look out for those Dark Bandits, Father Anderson." Morgan Le Fay warned Grandpa.

"Yes, Sophia told me all about them. Hopefully Lamorak scared them off for a while." Grandpa said.

"I hope so," said Guinevere.

With that they walked in the direction of Lamorak's castle.

~~~~~~

Casey Lane rode ahead of the King and his knights. Jennie and Leila rode beside her. They arrived where the attack had happened.

"Look at the graves!" Leila pointed as she screamed in horror!

"Oh no," said Jennie, "I hope it isn't any of our men!"

"Well, it has to be," said Richard riding up and jumping off his horse. "The enemy would have taken their dead with them. Our men weren't going home, they would have had to bury them."

Casey Lane jumped off her horse too, they looked around. There had been a horrible battle. She followed the hoof prints from the horses. There was something hiding behind a bush. She reached down and pulled out a phone! Then she went running back to the others.

"Look what I found!" Exclaimed Casey Lane excitedly!

"Oh, no!" Screamed Jennie putting her hands to her mouth. "That's Sophie's!"

Richard came over and put his arm around Jennie. "I'm sure she's ok, honey." He tried to comfort his wife.

King Arthur rode up.

"This is not good; men you need to dig up those graves. We need to see who's in there." He instructed his knights.

The knights jumped off their horses and went over to the graves.

"Not a pleasant task," said one of the knights.

"No, but we need to just get it done," said another.

They dug up the graves and then King Arthur went over to look inside them. He took count of which knights he had lost and said a prayer.

Casey Lane came up behind them and glanced in the graves too. Then she turned and walked back to Jennie.

"Sophie isn't there, so she's alive," said Casey Lane.

"Thank goodness!" Sobbed Jennie with relief.

The graves were covered back up and King Arthur ordered everyone to continue forward. No way were they going to camp here tonight.

26

THE NEXT morning Sophia begrudgingly left this oasis with her party. As Gunther flew them out she looked down at the sandy beach and sea cliffs. Wow, I could live here, she thought to herself, they flew all day and landed in Loch Ness that evening. Sophia made sure they stayed away from the water; she didn't want to meet any hideous sea monsters tonight!

~~~~~~~

Lamorak, Perceval, Accalon, and Lancelot were now riding through Ayr.

"Well, look at that!" exclaimed Lamorak.

"Yes, Merlin has been here for sure!" Laughed Perceval.

"Let's pass quickly before any more trolls not turned to stone show up!" Shouted Accalon.

They made their horses go swiftly through the stone trolls and ended up near Glasgow that night.

~~~~~~~

Grandpa, Jackie Lee, Morgan Le Fay, and Guinevere arrived at Lamorak's castle.

"Thank goodness the drawbridge is down," exclaimed Guinevere!

"Yes, I don't want to walk all the way to Camelot!" Said Morgan Le Fay.

They entered the courtyard and walked over to the stable.

"Hello, anyone around?" Asked Guinevere.

"Yes, hello," said a stable hand as he walked out to see what they wanted. He saw it was the Queen and dropped to his knees.

A kitchen hand was walking back into the kitchen when she noticed the crowd and realized it was the Queen.

"The Queen is here!" She shouted as she ran into the kitchen.

Everyone dropped what they were doing and ran out into the courtyard to see the Queen.

"I heard she's been missing," said one maid.

"Well look who she's with and look at that dog! He's wearing armor!" She giggled.

"Please get up," said Guinevere to the stable boy. "We need some horses or a carriage to get us Camelot tonight.

He got up and said, "the carriages have all been taken, but we have an open carriage in the back. Would that do?"

"Yes, that will be fine," Morgan Le Fay said rather tartly. She was getting impatient.

"Guinevere are you going with us to catch up to the King or are you going back to Camelot to stay?" Asked Grandpa.

"I want to go with you to find Arthur," she said.

"Morgan, what about you?" Asked Grandpa.

"Well, I'm not going to miss out on any fun!" she answered.

"Ok, then why don't I call Jennie and see where they are. I won't let them know I'm here, so we can surprise them." Grandpa told them.

"That's a great idea!" Guinevere said; she was getting excited.

"Well, let's leave here and I'll call. I don't want to draw any more attention to ourselves. If they have left on the trip, is there a short cut for us, so we don't have to go to Camelot?" he asked.

"Yes, we can take another road that goes north of Camelot and will save us a lot of time if we are going to Scotland." said Guinevere.

The carriage was brought out and the horses were hitched up. The kitchen maids loaded the carriage with baskets of food and water. The stable hand put enough oats in the back for the horses to keep them for a week. It was a huge carriage, so it could carry everything. They rode out of the castle and an hour later came to a fork in the road.

"Ok, let's pull up here," Grandpa said, they were at the intersection of either going to Camelot or taking the short cut to Scotland.

Ring ring, "Hello," said Jennie surprised to find her phone ringing.

"Hello dear, this is Grandpa," he said.

"Hi Grandpa, what's up?" asked Jennie.

"I was just wondering where you are dear? Have you started on your journey?" asked Grandpa.

"Yes, we're almost in Scotland," she answered.

"I will check in with you from time to time dear. Stay safe and let me know when you find your sister." He said.

"Ok, Grandpa, I will. You take care too. I love you," she said.

"Good bye dear, I love you too." With that he hung up with a grin on his face.

"This is going to be fun!" Exclaimed Guinevere joyfully, jumping up and hugging Grandpa.

"Yes, it is!" Grandpa beamed.

Jackie Lee barked, and Morgan rolled her eyes and laughed.

~~~~~~~

"I'm going back home!" Cundrie pouted, showing her anger and disgust to Iago. She was sitting next to a dumpster they had just rummaged through for scraps of food. They were behind a row of restaurants in down town Luxembourg.

"I don't think we had it this bad at home. Will I still have a job though?" Asked Iago.

"If I still have a marriage you will." She said tartly. She got up and dusted off her dirty skirt. Come on let's start walking to the caves.

Iago got up and followed her, feeling low about the situation they were in.

~~~~~~~

27

FROM LOCH NESS the next day Sophia and her party made it into the Northern Highlands.

"Are you getting close to home Gunther?" She asked the dragon when they stopped for a quick break.

"Yes, I believe so, aren't we Merlin?" asked Gunther.

"Looking at this map, I believe so. We need to go to the very tip of the Northern Highlands. Your family should be on one of the Orkney Islands. King Arthur found you as a baby in the Northern Highlands. Your parents were killed and taken by men that wanted to wipe all of you out. We saved you, I believe your remaining family would have moved as far north as they could for safety." Merlin replied.

"Well then we are almost there!" Sophia exclaimed with excitement. "Will they accept Kanani and me?" she asked.

"I think that Gunther and I should approach them first, Sophie. We will leave you on the mainland for a short while until we know it's safe." Said Merlin.

"NO!" Cried Gunther despairingly! "Sophie and Kanani must come with me!"

"Gunther, Merlin will protect you!" Sophia told him.

"You will be alone though, and something could hurt you!" Gunther cried.

She went over and gave that silly dragon a hug. "I love you too Gunther." she said.

"I love you too!" Gunther sobbed.

Sophie has me Gunther, I will protect her.

"Come on let's not waste good daylight," said Merlin.

"Ok," I said, "let's go Gunther."

Gunther got up and lowered himself, so they could all scamper up on him.

Gunther flew for a few more hours and then landed along the coastline for the night. Tomorrow they would reach the tip of the land, Dunnet Head, towards their destination.

~~~~~

Lamorak and the knights made it to Clyde River that night. They sat up camp and took turns keeping watch. In the middle of the night ugly trolls attacked them!

28

"WE'RE FINALLY here!" Sophia shouted with joy!

"I am so excited!" Stated Gunther nervously.

"Ok, why don't we land and walk around to find a good place to leave Sophie and Kanani, Gunther." Said Merlin.

Gunther landed; there were beautiful white sand beaches with limestone cliffs at Dunnet Head.

"Oh, look there's a huge cave, Merlin! Can we check it out?" Sophie asked him.

"Let me go first in case something lives in it Sophie." said Merlin.

He climbed down the cliff and proceeded to check out the cave. He was gone a long time. Then he appeared with a grin on his face just as Sophie was starting to get worried.

"It's empty, follow me." He said gesturing to follow him.

Kanani bounded down ahead of Merlin and Sophia climbed down behind him. Gunther flew and beat them all there. Beautiful eagles were flying around them. It was gorgeous here, but Sophie knew the weather in winter was cold.

"Kanani and I will be fine here Merlin. Do you want to stay one night or go over to the Islands right away?" she asked.

"I think we should go take a quick look and come back for you tonight Sophie. This cave is empty now, but who knows what animal lives here at night." he said.

"Then please go and hurry back," she said as she walked over to Gunther and kissed his face. "You'll be ok Gunther, I love you." she told him.

"I love you too," Gunther replied.

With that Gunther and Merlin took off and left Kanani and Sophia on the beach. They arrived on the little island of South Roanaldsay a short time later.

Gunther landed with Merlin and they looked around. Suddenly a white dragon came forward to see who had come for a visit. There were ten dragons, counting a baby dragon.

A big dragon came forward, the others stayed back.

"I'm Drake, who are you?" he asked Gunther.

"I'm Gunther, I live with King Arthur and this is his wizard, Merlin."

"Gunther!" Shouted Drake, your alive! I didn't recognize!" He bounded forward to hug Gunther. Merlin jumped off to get out of the way.

All the dragons introduced themselves to Gunther; Merlin took out his looking glass to check on Sophia and Kanani. To his horror he saw two big black dragons with something in their claws!

29

SOPHIA WAS watching Gunther and Merlin disappear. He wasn't paying attention to Kanani barking when she was attacked from above! A big ugly black dragon grabbed Sophia and another one snatched Kanani. Sophia started screaming while Kanani was barking and struggling.

Let me go you big bird! This is not supposed to happen!

Merlin left the dragons to use his eyepiece to check on Sophia and Kanani. He saw what happened and was horrified.

Merlin raced back to Gunther and shouted to all of the Dragons that he saw a black dragon grab Sophia and another one grabbed Kanani. They needed to go get them now!

"Ok, let's go kick some black dragons around and save our friends! Gunther you stay back with baby Fafnir and Merlin!" Drake shouted as they took off to save them.

"I'm not staying here, hop on Merlin. Fafnir stay with your mom." With that Gunther and Merlin took off behind the big white dragons.

Drake reached the dragon holding Sophia and attacked him from above. When that happened Sophia was let go so the black dragon could fight back. Sophia plunged to the ground but was saved by some brush and the fact that the black dragon was not too far airborne yet. Then another white dragon attacked the one holding Kanani. She dropped down next to Sophia. Sophia grabbed Kanani's collar and they ran as fast as they could in the opposite direction. Then they saw Gunther approaching.

"Sophie and Kanani, I'm coming for you!" Shouted Gunther so they could hear him. *I knew you would, Gunther. Hurry!* Kanani started barking.

Gunther made a quick landing and they climbed onto him. Merlin helped Sophia get on Gunther and then helped Kanani. As they took off they looked at the battle, the white dragons were winning. They flew back to the island and landed. The female dragons gathered around inquiring for their wellbeing. They couldn't believe what they had been through and neither could Sophia.

If they only knew what she and Kanani had really been through they would have been truly amazed. Sophia was wondering why she was here again. Thinking perhaps her thinking had been a bit off when she decided to come back in time once more.

It was hours before the male dragons came back. The female dragons had food out and Merlin made a huge bon fire to keep the humans warm that evening. There was a chill in the air as they sat around for most of the night talking. It was decided that they needed to stay here until backup knights arrived. The other hope was that King Arthur had gotten wind of their dire situation and would come to save them. The dragons were apprehensive at first to leave this place until Gunther convinced them they would be safer and happier with a life in Camelot. Sophia just kept thinking about the caves being prepared for them behind the town, hoping there would be enough of them for the ten dragons and Gunther too. How she loved that dragon! She could never go back to the future and leave him behind.

30

A BIG ugly smelly four-foot troll came stomping into camp. Lamorak pulled out his sword and swung at him. Perceval jumped up out of a light sleep and got behind him. The troll turned to face Perceval, and Lamorak swung his sword slashing his right arm. The troll screamed and grabbed his nearly severed arm turning to glare at Lamorak. Perceval used this opportunity to finish him off. Then there came two more trolls looking like the first one wanting to kill the men. This battle went on for an hour, when it was finished the brave knights were exhausted. At least they were all alive; the trolls had all been killed. The camp was a disaster, so they decided to pick up what they could and leave right away. It was now early evening and they arrived in Saint Andrews, they decided to rest up and eat. Tomorrow would be another long day, but they should be safe tonight. There were people around and a small village. They would be able to get some supplies that they had lost last night and stock up for the rest of the journey.

~~~~~~~~

Grandpa, Jackie Lee, Guinevere, and Morgan were making good time. They had not run into any trouble, and the short cut should bring them above the others. The King's party was so large they must be moving slow. They got onto the main road going into Scotland.

"Now we are either behind them or ahead," Grandpa told the others. "Let's camp here by the stream tonight and see if we hear anything in either direction tomorrow morning."

"I agree," said Guinevere, "I'm tired of riding in this carriage all day. She stopped the horses and they got out. Jackie Lee jumped out and went over to the water gulping it down. Grandpa unhooked the horses, got them watered and fed. Morgan actually made a place for them to eat and started a fire. They spent a pleasant uneventful evening; they didn't know how lucky they were, because they were just below the place that Merlin had turned the trolls into stone. They calculated that the King's band must be behind them, they had taken quite a short cut. They waited another day and then it happened. They heard voices and horses. Jackie Lee took off running fast towards the noise.

~~~~~~

Casey Lane thought she heard Jackie Lee. She was riding next to Jennie.

"Did you hear that?" She asked Jennie.

"Yes, that's strange. There aren't any dogs with us." Jennie said.

~~~~~~

Jackie Lee had spotted Casey and was barking his head off running as fast as his legs and body armor would let him. *Casey! Here I am, see me? I found you, I found you!*

~~~~~~

"Oh my gosh! That's Jackie Lee!" Screamed Casey Lane jumping off her horse and running to greet her dog.

When they met, Jackie Lee jumped up to greet her, as she bent over to pet him, he started licking her face.

"How did you find me? What a clever boy, I'm so happy to see you!" Casey Lane was beside herself with joy.

"Look, there's Grandpa too!" Screamed Jennie as she ran to hug her grandfather.

Guinevere stopped the horses and Grandpa jumped off taking after Jackie Lee. For such an elderly man he was still in pretty good shape.

"Grandpa! How did you find us? I can't believe you're here!" Cried Jennie finally reaching him and giving him a big hug.

"Jackie Lee and I could not stay away from this adventure, and neither could Morgan or Guinevere."

"Grandpa, that's awesome!" Jennie cried. Leila and Richard came running up to greet the newcomers too. They were all talking and hugging when King Arthur approached, everyone stopped talking and held their breath.

"Your Highness, your Queen awaits you," Grandpa told him with a twinkle in his eye.

"I see her, excuse me," King Arthur said as he took off to greet his wife.

He approached the carriage. "My Lady I have missed you." He said.

"I never want to leave you again, my King. Please forgive me, I have missed you too." Guinevere stepped out of the carriage and the King lifted her up to sit in front of him on his horse.

It was such a great reunion for all involved; they stayed there that evening. They talked into the night then decided how they were going to proceed on this quest.

31

CUNDRIE AND IAGO finally made it back to the caves. It was a long unpleasant journey that tired them both. Cundrie was in a foul mood and took it out on Iago.

"Ok, here we are." Cundrie said and gave Iago an exasperated look. "This is enough adventure for me, I will go first."

"That is fine, go ahead and I will be behind you."

With that Cundrie went through the portal and landed on the other side. She looked around, she was so happy to be back. She hoped that Accalon would not be too unhappy with her. Iago kept his word and came through a few minutes later.

"Ok," Cundrie looked at Iago, "We need to start walking to the castle before it gets dark."

"I don't know if I should go back, in fact I think I will go in the other direction." He started walking away from her.

"Oh no you don't! I did not get into this mess alone and I will not face Accalon or Yglais alone!" She was glaring at his disappearing back. "At least walk me back, so I am not alone!" She pleaded with some desperation in her voice.

He turned around. "Ok, I will walk you back, but I do not know if I shall stay."

"Good enough, I guess. Let us start off now." She said with relief in her voice.

He turned around, came back to her and they walked off side by side, not saying a word. After an hour they saw the castle. Cundrie was getting butterflies in her stomach with anxiety. Little did she know that Yglais, Accalon, Perceval, and Lamorak were not in Camelot. She did not have anything to be afraid of yet. They got closer and her mouth fell open.

"I can not believe this! Look, the drawbridge is up. We can not enter the castle!" Cundrie exclaimed.

"It is never up except at night, or if there is danger." He looked around. "We had better find cover before night comes. I wonder what is going on?"

"I don't know. I have an uneasy feeling. Perhaps we should get back on the road and keep walking towards Camelot. What do you think?" She asked him.

"Yes, we need to get out of here." He said, "First let us walk around the outside of the castle. I know another way in if it's unlocked."

"You do?" Cundrie asked. "Who else knows about this?"

"Merlin, I saw him using it one time when he was visiting. He did not see me watching him. Follow me and I will show you where it is." He turned and starting walking clockwise around the outside wall of the castle. The only problem was the moat around the castle. They would have to cross that first.

"What do you expect me to do?" Cundrie huffed at Iago. "Wade through that mucky infested water?"

"Do you have another idea? Really Cundrie this is not as bad as eating out of dumpsters." He kept walking around the outside of the moat glancing at the castle wall for the opening. She had to walk fast to keep up with him.

She thought that eating out of dumpsters was pretty disgusting when you were hungry, but it just might be beneath her to get in that murky water.

"Ok, there," he pointed, "Do you see the outline of the door?"

She squinted. "Yes, how do we know if we can enter through it?"

"We don't until we try." he said. "I will get into the water and go across. If it is unlocked I will come back and help you through the moat, ok?"

"Do I have a choice?" Cundrie sulked.

"Not unless you want to be a sitting target unprotected out here all night." He tossed off his jacket and removed his shoes.

She watched him wade in about 8 feet or so then it was really deep and he had to swim across the middle portion until he could wade out of the muddy water.

He made it to the other side. He got onto the bank and turned around throwing his hands in the air.

"See nothing ate me and I made it. You can do this too. Let me check the door." He shouted across the water.

He went over to the door and pushed on it. To his relief it swung open. He stepped inside. This passageway ran beneath the courtyard, under the castle coming out into the kitchen. He was satisfied they could get through or at least hide in here tonight until the castle was accessible in the morning. He stepped back out and swam back across to Cundrie.

"Ok, grab my hand and let's go." He said pulling her into the water.

"Oh, I hate this! The dumpster is fine dining compared to this." She moaned but followed him.

They made it across. She got out behind him and wrung out her dress then followed him through the door.

They walked through a long dark damp tunnel; she knew there were rats; she could hear their squeals and scuffling along the floor.

It seemed like forever before they came to stairs leading up. They reached the top of the 100 steps and there was another long staircase no different from the previous one.

"Do you know for sure where this ends up?"

"I have done this one other time and it comes out in the pantry of the main kitchen." He told her.

"Good, maybe we can get something decent to eat when we get there." She was really wet and cold, but above all she was famished. They had not had a decent meal in weeks. They should have stayed with the others at the monastery. Better yet, they should have never gone. "

Too late for that kind of thinking now. She thought out loud.

"Did you say something?" Iago asked.

"Ah no, just talking to myself she sharply said, while thinking the only intelligent conversation is one with herself."

"Ok, look there's the entrance up ahead." He hurried his steps.

"Thank goodness, I am worn out." She could hardly take another step.

Iago opened the door, there was no lock on it and they stepped through. The cooks were in the kitchen just sitting down with the hired help to eat. They saw Cundrie and Iago. Jumping to their feet, three of the women ran over to hug them.

"We have been so worried about the two of you. The Queen came through here not that long ago, we wondered where the two of you had gone." Said Ivis, the Head Cook.

"Come dear, sit by the fire," she grabbed Cundrie and walked her over to the open fire. Another servant grabbed two chairs. Both Cundrie and Iago were placed by the fire to dry out and given a big bowl of hot stew with homemade bread to eat.

"Is Sir Accalon or Lady Yglais here?" asked Cundrie.

"No, Lady Yglais is still at Camelot overseeing the houses being built. Sir Perceval, Sir Lamorak, and Sir Accalon went on a quest and never returned. So, King Arthur has a party going after them as we speak. There is no telling when they will return." said Ivis.

"They never returned? This is terrible!" Cundrie cried.

"Yes it is. They left to seek the last of the white dragons, to save them from extinction," added Afawen the maid.

"I must get to Camelot tomorrow," Cundrie said, "If anything has happened to Accalon I will never forgive myself for having left." She finished her stew and placed her dish in the sink. "Thank you for feeding me. I need to go to my room and get cleaned up. Please have a bath prepared. I will see all of you in the morning. Iago, take care and go to the stable. I will need a horse in the morning and I would appreciate it if you got my white horse ready by eight a.m."

"Yes, my Lady, I will have her ready. However, you cannot ride to Camelot alone." He looked around.

"I will go with you, my Lady," said Afawen. "Bryn went with Lady Sophia and I am not needed here. I can at least help Lady Yglais' maids get them settled in the new house. The plan is for us to take turns living in Camelot and running this castle."

"Good, I will ride with you too then," said Iago. "If anyone else is wanting to go, be at the stable early in the morning, so we can prepare the trip." With that he thanked them for the food and left.

32

CASEY LANE and Jackie Lee were riding ahead of the King's entourage. Jackie Lee started barking so Casey caught up to him to see what he was making such a fuss about.

"Jackie Lee, come here," she called getting off the horse.

Jennie was right behind her with Richard. They got off their horses as well and walked over to take a look at what was setting Jackie Lee off.

"What are they?" Asked Casey Lane.

"They look like stone trolls," said Richard. "Ha, Merlin must have been this way. He would not have left Sophia or Kanani, so I bet they're alright Jennie."

"I hope your right, Richard. How horrifying these trolls must be when alive!" Jennie was disgusted and walked away.

The Kings' party arrived and had a look around. It was decided that they should try to move on tonight and find a safer place to camp.

~~~~~~

Weeks had gone by and everyday Merlin looked through his eyeglass to see if anyone was coming for them. Then one morning he saw something!

33

MERLIN RAN back to get Gunther's attention.

"Sophia, Gunther, I just saw some knights. We need to go over to the mainland and have a look."

"Come on Gunther, let us get on you so we can go see who found us!" Sophia was so happy she wanted to jump for joy but climbed onto Gunther instead. Of course, Kanani had to go too, so Merlin helped her get aboard, then he got on and off they flew over the water.

The men were looking around and then noticed Gunther.

"Look, I think that's Gunther!" Shouted Perceval, he was thrilled!

"It is, there's Sophia and Kanani!" Lamorak shouted as he jumped off his horse.

Gunther flew over them. "It's our knights! You can land Gunther." Merlin instructed the dragon.

Gunther circled and landed by the men.

Sophia jumped off Gunther and Kanani did too following behind her.

"I can't believe you found us! I'm so happy!" She ran over forgetting her dignity and hugged each of the Knights.

"We are happier to see you," exclaimed Lamorak. "We have had a rough journey, it looks like you did too. We saw the stone trolls and the dead dragons. I'm amazed to see all of you alive. How did you defeat the black dragons?"

"We had help." Sophia continued relating the adventure they had along the way to find the white dragons."

"Where are the rest of you?" asked Merlin.

"They were killed, Merlin. It was a horrible battle. How many dragons have you found?" Lamorak asked.

"There are ten dragons, eleven with Gunther."

"Well that's too many dragons for us to take to Camelot alone. There are too many dangers."

"Lamorak, you four cannot stay here either unless the dragons come over here. Black dragons guard these beaches at night."

"Perhaps we should get the dragons to move over here," Perceval told them.

"Yes, I think that is the best idea," said Lamorak.

"Ok, then it's decided, if we can convince them. Let's talk to Gunther." Merlin turned around and walked over to Gunther giving him the men's suggestion.

"Ok, let's go back and talk to Drake and the others," agreed Gunther.

"Sophia, you and Kanani stay over here. Gunther and I will return with an answer or with dragons. Why don't you find a good place for eleven dragons and all of us," Merlin offered?

Sophia turned around and spoke to Lamorak. "There's Smoo Cave down below us. I would love to explore it. I think it's big enough for all the dragons and us too. That way we will have protection from the black dragons and plenty of food from the sea."

"That is an excellent idea. Can you show us where it is?" he asked her.

"Yes, just follow Kanani and me." Sophia started leading the way.

Lamorak turned back around, "Perceval, you and the others can follow us with your horses." Then he turned back around leading his horse behind Kanani down the trail.

We got down to the beach and approached the cave.

"Stay here Sophia, let us check out the cave first and make sure that there aren't any dragons living in it." Lamorak said.

"Ok, but I'm pretty sure it will be ok. The white dragons had a battle with them and won. The black dragons haven't been seen around since." Sophia told him.

The men left their horses outside and walked into the cave. Upon entering they saw what a wide cave it was, the chamber they walked into was about forty to fifty feet high, one hundred fifty feet long and a little more than 100 feet wide. This would be an excellent place to house all of them, even throughout the winter. They came out a bit later and Lamorak had a grin on his face.

"It is a grand cave, Sophia. You can get Kanani settled here. We will arrange for the horses to eat and start a fire. Perceval is already getting set up to catch some fish for our dinner."

"Fabulous! Come on Kanani!"

Ok, Sophie, this is fun! Can we eat now?

By the time they saw Gunther flying back with Merlin with other dragons flying behind him, they had a warm fire going. Dinner was made; a place for the dragons was set up in the cave.

There was a great introduction between the men and dragons.

~~~~~~

Cundrie, Iago and Afawen arrived in Camelot. Lady Yglais ran over to great them. She didn't know if she was angry with Cundrie or glad to see her. Cundrie was also apprehensive about the meeting. Lady Yglais interrogated both Cundrie and Iago until she was satisfied, and then laughed from relief. She had feared the worse for both of them. Iago was allowed to stay for now. They were to wait until Accalon arrived, if he came back alive it would be his decision. In the meantime, Iago was put to work getting the homes and caves ready for the hopeful return of the dragons and people.

~~~~~~

The Kings men were getting closer to the cave where Sophia and the Dragons were staying. They didn't know it though and with winter coming upon them the King feared they would be stuck with no shelter or food. They needed to get there soon or find a town to stay in and wait out winter

~~~~~~

The dragons were doing well sleeping with the humans in the cave at night. By day they went up the cliff, played, caught food and looked for any help coming to get them.

"Sir Lamorak," said Sophia, "I really want to explore this cave. I've checked and there are several tunnels and chambers. It would be fun to see where each of them go. Tomorrow Kanani and I are going exploring. I just wanted you to know so that you don't worry about us."

"Thank you for telling me, however I do not think it is safe for a Lady to go off on her own. Perceval and I will accompany you and Kanani." He was determined not to let Sophia out of site after that attack of the black dragons and not knowing what was in the tunnels.

"Great, do you think you should ask Perceval first though?" Sophia was being smart.

"Yes, I suppose I should," Lamorak laughed. "Come with me, let us find him and see if he will go on the mission quest with us."

With that Lamorak called Kanani and they climbed the cliff looking for Perceval.

Perceval and Lancelot were practicing swords fights. The dragons were cheering for one or the other of them. They had to keep themselves in shape.

It was agreed that the next day Perceval, Lancelot, Accalon, Sophia and Kanani would explore the caves. Merlin preferred to stay back and work on some magic, protecting the dragons too, in case any black dragons approached.

"After this Sophia, we must prepare for winter. I do not think any of the King's men will get here before the cold winds and temperatures arrive." Lamorak was looking a bit worried about this.

"Ok, I promise that I will help us get everything ready after this venture." Sophia agreed excitedly.

Smoo Cave is a very large sea cave; it has a cave river running through it and lies at the inner end of a narrow inlet with Durness Limestone. The layers in this formation are layers of limestone and dolomites. The birds she had seen in the cave were rockdoves, they nested in the higher chambers of the cave. There were starlings living in the holes within the rocks. There were wrens and blackbirds living at the cave mouth plus numerous other creatures. They had been eating a lot of rabbit lately. Sophie knew they couldn't live on just rabbit. They needed to find other sources of food, perhaps there were fish in the river. She was anxious to see the cave river she remembered reading about years ago. Sophia had a special love of caves and had done a thesis paper in college on the most famous caves around the world.

The next morning they got ready and explored through one of the tunnels. It was dark at first then they heard gushing water. They came into a massive cavern dimly lit with phosphorescence. They could just make out a pool of fresh water and a waterfall coming from above out of the limestone walls.

"Look, fresh water for us!" Sophia chased Kanani over to the water. Kanani barked and jumped in splashing all around. Yippee, water! Everyone started laughing, this was a good sign that they had some fresh water now.

"We will have to figure a way to get this water to all of us daily, it's too narrow in here for the dragons to get through the passageway. Let us move on and see what other wonders we can find in here." Lamorak led them out of this cavern back into the passageway.

They came to another cavern and it too had running water, which ran into the cave river she knew was here.

"This is what I wanted to find," she told the others.

"Wow, if we had a boat we could go down the river and see where it comes out." Accalon said.

"We might have plenty of time to build one if no one comes to help escort the dragons home soon," Lamorak answered him.

They spent a whole day walking down one passageway, before they knew it the day was drifting into evening and they needed to get back. Little did they know what they had missed that day, but they were about to find out.

34

THEY HEARD them before they saw them.

"Gunther come here please?" Merlin asked the dragon. "I sense someone approaching. Could you see who is coming please?"

"Yes, Gunther is a good dragon, I will be back." Gunther said as he took flight.

~~~~~~

"Look, that's Gunther!" Shouted Jennie to Casey Lane and Richard.

"So, it is! Fantastic, we made it!" Shouted Richard.

Jennie, Casey Lane, Jackie Lee and Richard let the King know. King Arthur was so relieved to finally arrive at their destination.

~~~~~~

Gunther saw them and flew back to Merlin. The dragons were all lined up with Merlin in front as the King's party approached. Jackie Lee was introduced to the dragons, so he didn't chase them. Sophia, Kanani and the others came out of the cave in time for the arrival of the King's party. They were greeted warmly by everyone! Sophia and Casey Lane shook hands; Kanani and Casey Lane chased each other. There was so much going on with all of the additional people. The King had his soldiers get water out of the cave; they had a lot of food and supplies, so they set up camp above the cave. Only the dragons would sleep in the cave from now on. They decided to bear out winter here and next spring they would make the long trip back to Camelot.

The winter passed, they made it through safely. Spring arrived so they started the long trip back to Camelot. Early summer was approaching when they reached their home. Word got around that the King was approaching. The King's people lined the pathway as King Arthur and his party approached. The people cheered and danced! A festival took place in honor of the dragons and the safe return of the King. This was a very long and successful quest.

The dragons were all given caves. Gunther had his cave closest to Sophia and Kanani.

"It's been a lot of fun," said Casey Lane. "Jackie Lee and I need to go home though."

"I understand, it was nice of you to come. I can't get over Jackie Lee convincing Grandpa to bring him through time. I will never stop chuckling about that." Sophia laughed.

"I know, Jackie Lee is quite the character." Casey Lane told her. It was so nice of your Grandpa to have me start calling him that too."

"I know, he is a dear," said Sophie.

Grandpa approached the women.

"I will go back with you my dear. You need to get your belongings from Sophia's house and then I will take you both to the airport after I pay you."

"Ok, sounds good to Jackie Lee and me." Casey Lane looked at Grandpa agreeing.

Grandpa turned to Sophia and Jennie, "I plan on coming back over here to live and open a Catholic Church. I'm going to become a Priest instead of a Monk. It will take a bit of time, but not much. Could you get the church built and a rectory for me?" He asked them.

"Yes, that's fantastic, Grandpa!" Sophia hugged him, Jennie got into the bear hug as well.

"Sophia and I will make sure it gets done, Grandpa, hurry back to us. I love you." Jennie said.

"I love all of you too, I will be back within the month." Grandpa then boarded the carriage with Casey Lane and Jackie Lee.

Bye, Jackie Lee, come back and see me sometime. It's been fun having another German Shepherd to talk to. Kanani told him.

Bye, Kanani. You're a fun girl too. This has been a grand time. I hope to visit again someday. Jackie Lee gave Kanani a lick and jumped into the carriage with Casey Lane and Grandpa.

The girls watched until the carriage was out of sight.

"Well, we have a lot more to do little sister. Let's get going." Jennie walked off to talk to the builders.

Sophia's house was done and so were Susan and Kimo's. They were cobblestone houses, with a kitchen, fireplace, living room, bathroom and two bedrooms. The roofs were thatch and Lady Yglais had flowers planted all around the front of Sophia's. Lady Yglais had her new place as well; it was much bigger than Sophia's, because she knew her son's would want to stay with her when in Camelot. Sophia found Yglais in the school putting all of Sophia's materials away on new shelves that had been built. School would start in the fall, Jennie and Susan would teach. Sophia decided to teach violin and work with the older children teaching them to read and write. Sophia and Lamorak were very good friends, it was an exciting time in Camelot. Guinevere had sent Lancelot away and the King was very relieved.

35

CASEY LANE, Jackie Lee and Grandpa went through the portal.

"I can't believe no one towed your car after all this time Grandpa."

"I had a monk from the monastery come put a sign in the window saying the car was not abandoned to call their number if it became a problem." Grandpa unlocked the driver's door and took down the sign. Then he unlocked the other doors letting Casey Lane and Jackie Lee in. When they arrived at Sophie's house, Casey Lane ran into the bedroom where her belongings were. Jackie Lee was hot on her heels. She grabbed her cell phone and turned it on.

"Yikes, Jackie Lee. Steven has left a lot of messages. Let's listen to them."

She pressed on the first message.

"Hi Casey, I got your message. Please call me when you and Jackie Lee return. Love Steve."

Message two, "Casey, I still haven't heard anything. I hope you and Jackie Lee are all right. Your house is fine. Please call me soon. Love, Steve."

Message three, "Casey, I'm getting really concerned. I know you are a big girl and know you can take care of yourself, well I think you can. I've got a big decision to make. I would love to discuss it with you. I need to talk to you soon. Please call me! Love, Steve."

Message four, "Casey, this must be some kind of case you're on. I hope Jackie Lee is taking care of you. I had to make the decision on my own. When you two come back here I will be gone. I took the Sheriff's job in a small town in Montana. I will keep this phone number. Please call me when you can. Maybe you and Jackie Lee can come visit me when you return? I love you Casey. Take care. Steve."

"Yikes! Steve moved to Montana Jackie Lee! With the money we made on this assignment we can go back to Seattle and buy an RV and drive to Montana."

That sounds like fun, whatever an RV is. Steve moved to Montana? Wow, I bet your upset Casey. Jackie Lee was thumping his tail and gave her his paw.

"Oh, thank you Jackie Lee." She took his paw and shook it.

~~~~~~

Grandpa walked out to the mailbox and returned to the kitchen. There was a letter from the government of the US State Department to Sophia. He wondered if he should open it and decided to call Sophia instead.

"Hi Grandpa, you made it back ok. I miss you already." Sophia told him.

"Hi dear, yes we made it back. Sophie, I'm calling dear because there is a letter here from the State Department to you. Do you want me to open it and read it you?" He asked her.

"Yes, it could be important."

Grandpa carefully opened it.

Dear Mrs. Sophia Barnes,

We have some news about the missing men from the mission your husband was on. We have found out that some of the men have survived but have been held by the Taliban. We don't want you to get up your hopes that Mr. Barnes is still alive, but it could be a possibility. We have a special investigation going on in this matter. You will be contacted if your husband is found alive. I'm sorry this has been so hard on you and the other families.

Thank you very much,

Colonel McFarland

"Good grief! What should I think?" Sophia asked her Grandpa.

"Don't get your hopes up dear. I will write a letter, with your help, right now to leave here in case John shows up. Then he will know where to find you. I will also leave a phone for him to call you."

"Thank you, Grandpa. I don't know what else we can do." Sophia told him. "I would like the letter to say this:"

Dear John,

If you are reading this letter, I know you are alive and have found your way home. I have loved you since the first time I saw you, I miss you more than you could ever know. My heart has been broken, but I can't hang on forever, Honey. I have an unbelievable story to tell you. In short, I'm with my sister and her husband. I've made a new life here; we are in Camelot. If you are alive, please call me. I will either come back for you or tell you how to find me if it is within 10 years' time. I pray it's you who is reading this.

Your loving wife,

Sophia

Grandpa wrote the letter while Sophie dictated it.

"Ok dear, I'll leave it on the counter. I love you Sophie, I'll check on the house from time to time until I come back."

"Thank you, Grandpa. I love you too. Goodbye for now."

"Goodbye dear." Then he hung up.

"Kanani, John might be alive." She said hopefully to Kanani.

Oh, Sophie don't get your hopes up. Kanani wagged her tail.

"I don't think I will say anything to the others, but I'm going to tell Gunther. Come on Kanani." Sophia got up from her desk and put her manuscript away. Kanani followed Sophia out of the house and over to Gunther's cave.

"Hi Sophie," Gunther came out to greet them. "Hi Kanani."

"Hi Gunther," she said.

Kanani wagged her tale and said in doggie talk, hi Gunther.

"I have come to give you some news. My husband may be alive!" Sophie told him.

"What do you mean might?" He was shocked and a little disappointed. Gunther didn't want to lose Sophie or Kanani.

Then Sophie explained about the letter and what it meant. She told him that it was a secret and Gunther liked that. They then said their goodnights.

~~~~~~

"Let's get our stuff together so Grandpa can take us to the airport, Jackie Lee."

Great I'm ready lets go. Jackie Lee was walking to the bedroom door.

"Wait a minute young man." Casey told him. "You remember what we went through at the Seattle airport with that body armor you insisted on wearing? Off it comes, I'll pack it in my suitcase."

No Casey I like wearing it. Jackie Lee gave Casey the cocked head sad eye look.

"Come here, I'm taking it off. We want to get home without any hassles." She walked over and took his armor off and put in her case. Then she gave Jackie a big kiss on the top of his head.

Ok, I like those kisses. Just this once Casey I will let you have your way. Thump thump thump, went Jackie Lee's tail.

~~~~~

It was possible to change history, if only in fairy tales. Sophia sat down at her new oak desk and continued writing her story about Camelot and the Dragon. She was writing a book for the school children. She would always wonder now, if someday John would show up. She felt truly blessed to have such a loving family with her in Camelot.

The End

Read on to get a taste of another exciting
adventure by J.M.M. ADAMS

The Mystery of St. Moritz

A Casey Lane and Jackie Lee GSD Mystery

1

"JACKIE LEE, COME here boy, let me take your scarf off."

Casey reached down and untied my scarf, and then she took her water bottle and doused it with water. After that she tied it over my nose and behind my head. It made the breathing a bit easier. She then did the same for herself.

It was pitch black, the building we were in was on fire, the door was jarred or something because we couldn't get out.

There was a sound!

"Casey, Jackie Lee!!! Are you in there? Can you answer if you are?"

Casey looked at me, "It's Peter and T.J., and they found us!"

"Peter, here we are!!!!" Casey yelled, then she grabbed my harness and we stumbled towards his voice.

Peter was hammering the wall; he finally broke a hole in it, and then tore the wood away. He stepped in with T.J. in front and shined a flashlight on us.

"Are you ok?" He asked Casey as she stumbled into his arms.

"Thank you for coming after us, please get us out of here."

"No problem, I'm glad we got here in time to save you." Peter said.

The flames were engulfing the building as he pulled Casey out, I followed T.J.

Hey buddy, that's twice in two years I owe you for saving our lives. I barked.

No trouble, we need to work together now more than ever. I followed your trail and led Peter to you. T.J. barked.

"Ok pups, stop barking until we get safely out of here, let's hurry." Peter had turned back to tell us to be quiet.

We ran down the hill away from the fire and piled into the Jeep, Captain was guarding the vehicle, and we were in danger!

In the Jeep as Pete drove us away, he looked at Casey, "The door was padlocked from the outside, you've gotten too close to the killer; we can't go home, a friend lent us her chalet to hide in."

The road got narrow and we were climbing the mountain.

"We're close to whoever is killing the horses competing in the 'Gubelin Grand Prix of St. Moritz.' The prize money is 135,135 Swiss francs, which comes to something like $138,500 dollars, plus fame and recognition. All I can say is thank goodness for T.J. being so good at scent and finding us." Casey replied.

"Casey, T.J., Captain and I want to join you and Jackie Lee, the GSD Agency, and be a part of your team. I don't need the money and you know I don't need to work. You wouldn't either if you'd marry me." Peter was concentrating on the road.

I think he was serious but of course Casey didn't jump with an answer.

Casey looked at him, "Why Peter, that's a funny way of asking me."

"Well, you're so busy I haven't had time to make it romantic, but I can tonight." He grinned at her.

"Let's get to the place and get cleaned up, all I can smell is smoke."

Peter told her, "That place is toast behind us; they meant to kill you and Jackie Lee! I'm not going to let that happen on my watch."

Casey squeezed his arm; "You and T.J. are definitely our hero's."

Then Peter, keeping his hands on the steering wheel and navigating the windy, muddy and curvy road up to the chalet said, "Casey, the first time I saw you on Sandy Island and I looked at you, then met you, my heart melted, and I fell in love with you. You have brought fun, happiness, adventure and life back into my life and T.J.'s too. You melt my heart and you're the smartest, kindest person I could ever want to know. The way you look at Jackie Lee and all of our dogs I see the person you really are. It makes me love you even more. These last couple of months here in Switzerland with you have made me look at myself even more. I will make it special when I ask you."

Well it's about time, I barked to T.J.

Woof! T.J. answered.

Casey looked at us and laughed.

"Peter, that is the kindest thing anyone ever said to me, except for Steve right before Jackie Lee and I were thrown out of the airplane in that horrible storm. So, hold on to that thought because I think there's trouble ahead!" Casey grabbed the dashboard.

"No kidding, what are all of the police doing?" Peter pulled the Jeep over to the side of the road and rolled down his window.

The policeman approached, "Sir, you can't pass this way, there's a hostage situation."

He pointed down the road, "If you go back about a mile, there's an access road to the chalets up the hill. Take a left and follow the road up, you will miss this mess."

"Thank you, sir." Peter rolled up the window and started backing down the hill.

The wind was howling, and dusk was falling, the trees threw a shadow over the road, Peter took it slow, it seemed like forever, but we finely made it up to our chalet. Peter pulled in the driveway and let us out. We got inside the chalet, it was an A Frame; and I couldn't see much because it was too dark. Peter flipped the light switch.

"No power Casey, I have a flashlight in the Jeep let me go get it for you and I'll get the fire going. It's nice they have wood stacked on the porch." Peter came back and handed the flashlight to Casey.

"Thank you, Peter, let me hold the flashlight for you until you get the fire going."

"Thank you, Casey, let's find some lanterns after I light the fire."

The fire was lit; there were lanterns in every room. Peter lit them, it was pretty cozy, then Peter took us dogs into the kitchen and fed us while Casey showered and changed. She joined us all refreshed, Peter set out crackers, cheese, salami and wine on a table in the living room. He and Casey sat on the big cozy chair by the fire, I stuck close to Casey, Captain was over by the fire and T.J. was in between Casey and Peter's legs on the throw rug.

"Casey, you and Jackie Lee could have been killed if we hadn't arrived in time. Please tell me how the two of you got trapped in that building." Peter took a sip of his wine, there was still no power.

"There was a letter addressed to me under our front doormat this morning. You were already gone, I opened it and it said that someone had information to the whereabouts of the killer. I left Captain to watch the villa, T.J. was off with you, so I left that note you found from me with the address we were going to and Jackie Lee and I took off. We got to the meeting place, it was an old warehouse, the door was opened, and the light was on. I stopped at the door, said hello and we stepped inside. As soon as we did the door slammed, I turned to push it back open and couldn't budge it, and then the lights went out. I was really frightened; I held on to Jackie Lee and walked along the wall looking for a way out. That's when we smelled smoke! I covered our faces with the handkerchiefs after soaking them in my drinking water. That's when you saved the day making a hole in that wall to get us out! I've never

been so frightened in my life!" Casey grabbed Peter's hand, "we need to narrow this down."

"Casey, they know where we live, that's why we are staying here; in the morning we'll go back to our villa and get a list of all of the neighbors. Someone knows something. I'm ready to pull you out of this mystery, it's gotten too dangerous."

"Peter, we need to solve it, no more horses need to die or disappear!" Casey sounded determined not to quit.

Everything went smoothly that night, to my relief no big events happened. The next morning all of us piled into Baron's truck. We headed back to the place we went yesterday. Baron stopped at all of the local places and asked if anyone had seen new people, anything strange lately, his horse. He showed her picture all around. Then we unhitched the horse trailer and took the truck up the road to the house. We looked through the windows of the house, no one was there, the barn was the same. Then I saw something we hadn't noticed yesterday!

"Five top contender horses have been eliminated by either disappearing or poisoning. The big event takes place in four weeks. We need to figure out if it's another contender doing this or someone else. We've visited with the owners, we've covered all of the questions, like is it a disgruntled jockey or trainer. No one has admitted anything. We're meeting Andre in the morning at our villa; he's the retired police chief that I introduced you to when we first arrived. The police department has brought him back in to help on the case. I went to the police station this morning for a meeting, I'm now a deputy." He reached in his pocket and took out a badge, "I don't want you or Jackie Lee to go anywhere without me knowing until this case is solved."

"That's impressive," Casey took it and checked it over, then handed it back. "Any suggestions?"

"Andre has some, we'll find out in the morning, we might as well get to sleep early, there's no electricity anyway." Peter got up and took Casey's hand, "Come on, I'll put you and Jackie Lee in your room. I'm sleeping out here with Captain and T.J."

"Just let me take a lantern and I'll find my way." Casey hugged him, "Good night."

"Good night Casey and Jackie Lee." Peter rubbed my head, "Look after our girl tonight kiddo."

I wagged my tail and followed Casey into a dark bedroom; I jumped on the bed and waited for her, not a bad mattress. Before I knew it, I was sound asleep.

Casey had her arm resting over my shoulder and I felt secure, I might have been snoring. Casey usually pokes me if I snore, but after the day we just completed another surprise would be too much.

Then it happened!

Our window shattered!

JMM ADAMS

2

"JACKIE LEE!" CASEY shot out of bed and looked at me in the dark, "what happened?"

Before I could answer, Peter came busting in through the door, shining his flashlight all around the room.

"Stay there Casey, in fact, get back on the bed and get off on this side, you too Jackie Lee. The window is shattered and glass is everywhere!"

"What happened?" Casey asked Peter.

"I'm not sure how this happened; we'll have to wait until morning. I'll call Andre first thing and let him know about this. Come with me, all of us can sleep by the fireplace in the living room." Peter took Casey's hand and I followed.

I found a cozy rug and snuggled up in it, soon asleep. I was just too tired to stay awake and to listen to Casey and Peter's conversation.

The next morning power was back on, Peter went outside and looked at the window from the outside, I went with him, T.J. came along and so did Captain. Peter saw footprints under the window, so he kept us back. He took out his phone and called Andre. He told him what had happened, then hung up.

"Let's go tell Casey, the police are coming out to get footprints and see what they can come up with." Peter hurried back around the house.

"Andre's coming sweetie, let's look in the phone book for a window repair person." Peter took off his coat.

"I have the phone book right here and found three possible companies, do you want me to go down the list and start calling?" Casey asked.

"Please and I'll fix everyone breakfast." He walked past her and kissed her cheek.

I followed T.J. into the kitchen; Captain was already waiting for breakfast.

Captain has sure gotten his confidence hasn't he T.J.?

You bet, it's great. It's good we get along with each other too. T.J. answered.

Why not get along? It's such a drag to be jealous of each other. Casey and I have seen dogs fight in a family and it just isn't my motto. I told him.

I've always been an only dog, so this is fun having others to go on adventures with. T.J. barked.

"Guys, you have a lot to say this morning, want to share it with me?" Peter laughed as he placed our dishes down for us to eat.

I just wagged my tail and gobbled my food.

Casey walked into the room, "The glass company will be here shortly and repair the damage. Do you need to let your friend know?"

"He's in Spain right now; I'll tell him when he gets back. Let's clean up the glass in the room after we eat and get this day going." Peter handed Casey some coffee.

"Deal." Casey said.

"I need to contact the race commission and let them know what has happened, too. They won't be too happy about this." Casey added.

"After we get back to the villa, why don't you do that Casey?"

"Ok," she answered.

The police came and took photos of the footprints, the glass people came after they left and repaired the window. Then we piled in the Jeep and Peter drove us to his villa to meet Andre, and for Casey to make her phone call.

On the way up to our villa I looked at the neighbors, there were two on the left and three on the right. The closest to Peter's house on the right was a little Bavarian Villa; a retired school teacher lived there with her cat. She was a sweet little old lady; she liked us and brought treats over all of the time. The house next to her house was empty, a vacation rental. The one next to that one on the bottom of the hill had a young man that was a chef at the Hotel Eden, St. Moritz renting the place. He worked a lot and probably didn't have anything to do with skiers. The two houses on the left of the road were a mystery to me. Peter and Casey needed to check them out though. It had to be someone close by that was trying to kill us. Someone had tabs on our actions and what we were doing. Now the place we stayed last night wasn't safe, so Peter

decided that staying at his place was best. He knew the inns and outs of most everyone around his place.

Andre met us right after we arrived. Introductions were made all around, and then Casey asked him a question.

"Andre, can you fill us in on anything with this horse race?"

"I would be delighted to my dear." Andre took a seat.

He was a big guy, white hair, dressed in snow boots, a big black parka, ski pants and he had a big moustache.

"Let me get you some tea," Casey said, "don't start until I get back."

She hurried back and handed the cup to Andre.

"Thank you dear, let's see, oh yes, the race. This is a race that people from all over the world will attend; fine thoroughbreds from all over Europe and international jockeys come to take part in the races at White Turf St. Moritz. The race is on the frozen Lake of St. Moritz, it's an amazing scene with the magnificent mountains in the background. Engadine Valley is amazing and beautiful. There is no other race like this one in the world! Men on skis are pulled along a track by unsaddled Thoroughbreds at speeds of up to 50 km/h. The race is over a period of three Sundays. There are other races as well, but this one is the unique one. There will be a tent city covering 130,000 square miles of the iced over Lake of St. Moritz.

This is not only a race! But a social and sporting event that with people from all over coming here. There will be two grandstands that will hold 2,000 people; therefore, many food vendors will make money.

The cash prizes are very generous; the prize money totals up to half a million Swiss francs. This is called the "European Cup on Snow." It's the most highly prized race in Switzerland! It has been going on for almost 100 years!" Andre proudly finished speaking and took a sip of his tea.

"That's amazing, someone wants that money bad enough to sabotage the other competitors!" Casey was amazed.

So was I.

"Excuse me a minute while I make a phone call." Casey got up and left the room, when she got back she said, "They want me to be in touch, I didn't tell them the details of what happened to us today though."

"I agree." Peter looked worried.

"We need to go back to the barns and mingle; we need to watch anything suspicious that is going on. It is a good idea to have T.J. and Jackie Lee there to keep an eye on people; you should have Captain on a leash and keep him with you for protection." Andre stood up, "Shall we depart? I have my truck outside; we can go in that unless you want to follow me in your Jeep?"

"We'll follow you in case Casey needs to bring the dogs back before we're done, Andre." Peter said.

"Just follow me then." Andre walked out and we followed.

He took us to the makeshift stables; it was fascinating walking through the busy barns. Casey and Peter met some interesting people. T.J. and I wandered around and kept our eyes on anyone suspicious.

I was walking by a paddock with T.J.; we were three barns back from Casey when we heard something! I walked a little faster, T.J. was right behind me. The door was open and someone was in a stall, he was bent over and he had sprinkled something in the water dish!

I barked and jumped on him, knocking him over!

The guy screamed!

T.J. get Peter, Casey or Andre, hurry, I'll hold him.

Right away Jackie Lee!

T.J. took off, the trainer came in.

"Get this dog off me!!!" Screamed the guy.

The trainer took his stick and started swinging it at me. I growled and showed my teeth.

He backed off and called for help.

"What's going on here?" Andre appeared with T.J.

"Get that dog off the man!" Shouted the trainer glaring at Andre.

"Put your stick down! Jackie Lee is a good dog and he sensed something wrong!" Andre rushed passed the trainer. The trainer lowered his stick and backed out of the stall.

"Good job Jackie Lee." Andre came over and put cuffs on the guy, I let go of him.

"This dog was just doing his job," Andre told the trainer. "I suggest you have that water tested now! I think Jackie Lee found this guy doing something in here that shouldn't have been done."

"What do you mean?" The caretaker was getting red in the face. "If this man has done anything to hurt my horse I'll press charges!"

He turned, "Johnny, get a fresh bucket of water in here now!"

The young boy ran off to do as he was told.

"Can you take that bucket out? I need to take a sample of the water to the station and have it tested. I'm Andre, a policeman."

"Yes, sorry, I'm Francois, one of the caretakers of Carson City Spirit, she has a good chance to win this event and if anything were to happen to her, I don't know what I'd do? The owners will be very upset about this. I don't know who this man is."

"I'm taking him down to the station to find out. You must have Carson City Spirit guarded by someone you strongly trust, whoever is doing this is going to try again to harm her. Thanks for the water." Johnny sat down the container of water for Andre to take with him.

"I will contact the owners and we will move her, putting a guard on her." Francois was furious.

Peter and Casey showed up, Peter took the crook from Andre.

"Jackie Lee, good boy!" Casey hugged me.

"Casey, why don't you follow us to the station, I'll ride with Andre and we'll talk after that." Peter patted my head.

"Good job Jackie Lee!"

I gave him high five.

It was a good feeling to get him, Peter.

"I'm sure I understood that bark Jackie Lee," Peter laughed.

"Come on Jackie Lee, T.J. and Captain, let's go, I'll see you down at the station." Casey said looking back at Peter.

We got to the station and the suspect was put into a cell. Andre filled out the paperwork and then came back out to meet Peter and Casey. We made it to the station before them and I was inside with Casey; T.J. and Captain were in the Jeep outside waiting for us.

"This is looking more and more like an inside job, we'll have the test's back this afternoon from the lab. Casey, whoever is plotting this will not stop at killing anyone! I know you were hired by the committee of this event to keep it safe, but I'm imploring you to let them think you are, but don't report everything we find to them. There is a leak on the inside; it isn't an outsider doing this. Can you do this?" Andre asked Casey.

"Yes, I have to agree with you. We are in grave danger and I believe that now Carson City Spirit is the horse they are going to do away with unless we stop them!" Casey looked at me.

"I'm worried about the danger to our dogs though." Casey added.

"That is why I'm telling you not to go anywhere or be left alone. You must insist Jackie Lee does not take off to solve this crime on his own." Andre told her.

Casey looked at me and shook her head, "Do you hear what he just said, Jackie Lee?"

Woof! *I hear you but it won't happen if any of us are in danger.* I barked at her.

"Well, Jackie Lee had a lot to say." Peter laughed.

"I don't think he agreed." Casey told him.

"Regardless, we are in agreement? Yes?" Andre asked.

"Yes," Casey and Steve both said together.

We said our goodbyes, decided to meet again after lunch.

I jumped into the Jeep next to T.J. and told both of the dogs what had happened. T.J. gave me a high five; we were going to solve this together!

Peter pulled up in front of St. Moritz Grill, "I'll go in and order food to go Casey, then we can go back home and eat. That way the dogs won't get cold waiting for us."

"Great idea, hold on. Casey looked the menu up on her I-Phone. Hmmm, how about an order of Red Crab Cake and an order of the Wood-Grilled Shrimp Cocktail for us to share and then look here," she showed him the menu, "do you want to share an entrée?"

Peter looked, "Yes, let's get the crab cake and shrimp dishes, then I would like the Turkey Panini or the Cuban Panini, which one?" Peter asked Casey.

"The Cuban Panini." She smiled at him, "I know how you love those."

"Ok, I'll be right back." Peter left the Jeep running so we would be warm and went inside. He came back out in twenty minutes with yummy smelling food.

I licked my lips. Casey took the sack from Peter and looked at me. I'll fix you guys a snack back at the villa, Jackie Lee." Casey laughed and turned back around.

They let us out at the villa and I jumped out relieving myself, and then ran into the house to join the others.

After lunch, Peter told us that we had better stay home, he was going to take Casey back to the stables and we could watch the house. I really knew that he didn't trust us not to get into some trouble.

So, Casey told us to be good and left with Peter. As soon as the door was shut, I turned to the others. We need to find out who tried to kill Casey and me, who's in?

I'm in! T.J. barked. We both looked at Captain.

Maybe I should stay here? Captain barked.

Probably a good idea, you can protect the place, we'll be back before Casey and Peter. Follow me T.J. I trotted off toward the garage, I slipped through the kitchen door and T.J. followed. The garage had a button to open the door and I hit it with my paw. Up went the garage door. I couldn't close it from the outside, oh well, Captain was in the house to protect it. T.J. and I took off across the yards, a shortcut to the stables.

Finally, at the stables we entered the aisle that Carson City Spirit's stall was in yesterday. It was empty.

I heard someone talking and coming our way. Hurry T.J. in here!

We flew behind the storage door across from Carson City Spirit's stall.

We listened.

"That pesky German Shepherd has to be caught and gotten rid of." One man was saying.

My eyes grew huge and I looked at T.J. *He's talking about me!*

I know, listen. T.J. said.

We listened more intently.

"We could have drugged and horse napped Carson City Spirit except for that dog! They have her under guard night and day now; I don't know how we can get her alone?" The same man said.

"We could drug the guard, or kill him." Another man said, who had a deep husky voice with a German accent.

"It would be too suspicious after trying to kill that dog and woman yesterday. I don't want to be caught." The first man said.

They weren't saying their names and I couldn't get a glimpse of them without revealing our identity.

"If we don't let him know who drugged him, we don't have to kill him. I'm not doing this for that reason. We need the horse until after the race and we'll hold her for ransom. That way Native Bid will win, we'll put all our money on him and then get a bonus from the owner for training him so well!" The first man said.

"Ok, so here's the plan........

I looked at T.J. We didn't hear the plan but we found out it's the trainer for Native Bid! Let's go find Casey; they plan on horse napping Carson City Spirit!

Jackie Lee, how do we convince Casey and Peter to understand what we just heard?

We can't so maybe we had just better try and find out where Carson City Spirit is being held to help her!

Great idea! T.J. barked.

I stuck my head out the door and looked, the coast was clear. We got out of the aisle and walked like we were supposed to be there until we came to the last row of stalls in Aisle Ten. I stopped in my tracks and T.J. almost ran into me. I looked both ways; our only hiding place was under the horse trailer. I dashed under it and T.J. followed.

That was close! T.J. barked.

Too close, there's Casey and Peter talking to the owner of Carson City Spirit.

"I have a guard on her around the clock, when she goes out to practice she's got a crowd around her, so she's as safe as I can keep her. She has a good chance at winning the race and I want her to be safe." Baron Aldman, the owner of Carson City Spirit told Casey and Peter. "I want to thank you for saving her the other day and I'm sorry you were almost killed the other day."

"You're most certainly welcome, and thank you, that was a horrifying experience! Peter and T.J. saved us. I'm forever thankful." Casey added looking at Peter.

"It's my concern they will kill whomever gets in their way and if they get to Carson City Spirit, it's all over. Do you trust your trainer?" Peter asked Baron Aldman.

"I do, his name is Marchion Hemburg, his father was my trainer before him. I have known him since he was a young boy, he is like family. Marchion grew up around my horses and he has always been honest and dependable. He wants for nothing, because I treat him very well. Do you think he is in danger as well?" Baron Aldman asked.

"I think we are all in danger, even you. I want a guard on you as well as Marchion." Peter told him.

Baron turned around and said, "Follow me, I'll make a call and hire some guards right now."

With that they disappeared from our view and hearing range.

Let's get back home before they do T.J. We have to figure out a way to tell Casey and Peter what we know.

I have an idea Jackie Lee, if we go right now up to them and let them know we are here then they will think that maybe we know something. If they just see us at home, they will think we have been home and know nothing new.

You're right T.J.! Let's go find them now!

We crawled out from under cover of the horse trailer and ran into the aisle looking for Casey and Peter.

Casey's eyes got big when she saw us. "Jackie Lee! T.J.! How did you get here?"

Woof woof! I said wagging my tail.

Peter turned to Baron and said, "These are your real detectives, let us introduce them."

Casey said, "This is Jackie Lee." I gave him a high five. Baron laughed.

Then Peter said, "Let me introduce you to T.J." T.J. offered his paw.

"Well, let me say, this is a delight to meet both of you. How much did you hear and where have you been? I bet you know something to help us."

Baron was intuitive, I must say. If only we could tell him what we know.

Baron made his call to hire guards then told us he was going to stay in his office until his hired guard appeared. He thanked us, Peter and Casey exchanged numbers, T.J. and I got a ride home with Peter and Casey.

As we approached Peter's place, he said, "Look at that Casey, they opened the garage door to get out."

"I think we had better start taking them with us," Casey laughed. "I bet poor Captain is frightened.

We got out the Jeep and piled into the house. Captain was whining and very happy to see all of us.

That night I had a dream.......

I was on a train, it was going fast, I had been put on it but all I could see was Casey Lane running after me as the train went faster and faster; she disappeared, and all my hope was gone.

Casey shook me awake. "Jackie Lee you were howling; it was just a bad dream boy. I'm here."

I licked her and fell back asleep into her arms. It wasn't long after that we heard the phone ring. I heard Peter answer it and then he came running into our room.

"Casey!" she sat up in bed.

"What is it Peter? Casey asked worriedly as she slipped out of bed into her slippers, and then grabbed her robe.

"That was Baron, Carson City Spirit's guard was just found dead and she is gone!"

ABOUT THE AUTHOR

MICHELE WRITES UNDER the pen name of JMM Adams. She lives in the North West with her beloved German Shepherds, Horse and parrot. A new book will be out next year, it's a mystery with Casey Lane and Jackie Lee. Casey Lane finds out some dark secrets about her grandfather and in seeking the truth, she puts herself and Jackie Lee in jeopardy.

Be sure to catch all the blogs and updates on new material on Facebook under Author J.M.M. Adams, twitter and www.jmmadams.com

Look for the Casey Lane and Jackie Lee books, they have many mystery's to solve……..

Also, war dog hero stories coming soon. War dogs from Iraq, Kuwait and Afghanistan. The *White Dragons of L'Azure* will be out next year.

92226042R00124

Made in the USA
San Bernardino, CA
31 October 2018